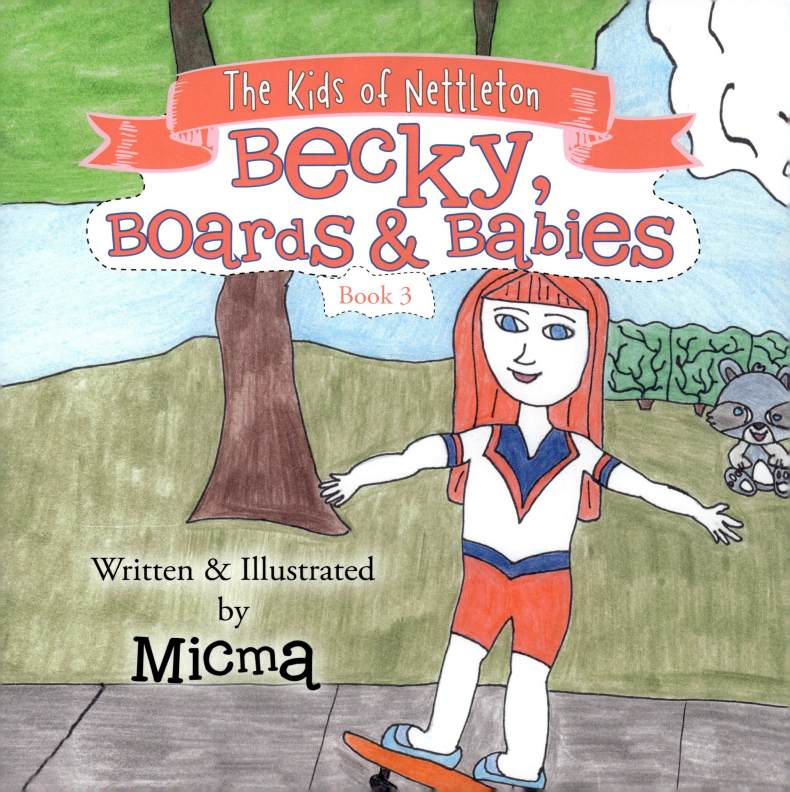

AuthorHouse™
1663 Liberty Drive
Bloomington, IN 47403
www.authorhouse.com
Phone: 1 (800) 839-8640

Published by AuthorHouse 06/12/2018

ISBN: 978-1-5462-4401-1 (sc)
ISBN: 978-1-5462-4402-8 (e)

Library of Congress Control Number: 2018906550

Print information available on the last page.

Any people depicted in stock imagery provided by Getty Images are models,
and such images are being used for illustrative purposes only.
Certain stock imagery © Getty Images.

This book is printed on acid-free paper.

Because of the dynamic nature of the Internet, any web addresses or links contained in this book may have changed
since publication and may no longer be valid. The views expressed in this work are solely those of the author and do
not necessarily reflect the views of the publisher, and the publisher hereby disclaims any responsibility for them.

authorHOUSE®

The Kids of Nettleton

Becky, Boards & Babies

Book 3

This book is dedicated to Becky Gall

A special "Thank You" to my lifelong friend and childhood 'sister' for allowing me to share your wonderful memories. You have provided insight for me to revisit my younger years while writing your story, and I appreciate it so much! If only my memory was as good as yours!

Micma

Chapters

May 1975

Chapter One

Summer Begins

"Cinderella dressed in yella,

Went downstairs to kiss a fella,

Made a mistake and kissed a snake,

How many doctors did it take

1, 2, 3..."

Becky jumped as Shari and Judy swung the rope.

"...27." Becky tripped but grinned. "That's my best yet!"

Shari took Becky's place, and the chant started over.

"I need a break," Becky told Sivi as she sat beside her on the step of the Hamilton Elementary School.

"Are you ready for summer?" Sivi asked.

"Yes and no," Becky replied. "I like school, but I look forward to sleeping later in the mornings, too," Becky replied.

"I know," Sivi nodded. "All of our friends are here, but..."

Becky patted her friend on the shoulder. "We will see each other this summer. There's the parade and swimming lessons. We can call each other."

"True," Sivi agreed.

Mrs. Moran blew the whistle. "Line up!"

The second-grade class followed their teacher to the restrooms and water fountains in the basement.

Becky was washing her hands when she noticed Judy waiting behind her. "Are you riding the bus home, or is your mom picking you up today?"

"I'm riding the bus." Becky moved aside for Judy to use the sink.

"Today we go to the Tastee Freeze on the bus after school," Becky reminded Judy. The two girls always sat together on the bus.

"I know," Judy licked her lips. "Yum. Vanilla ice cream cones are a great start for the summer."

"Chocolate would be better," Becky said. "Chocolate ice cream is my favorite."

"Mine, too. But vanilla still tastes good."

"You betcha!"

Mrs. Moran led the class upstairs. "Everyone needs to empty their desks. Don't forget to get your artwork from the wall in the hallway."

"There's the buses," Scotty called from his place by the window.

The kids rushed around packing their bags.

"I'll see some of you for summer school. Otherwise, have a great summer and I'll see you in September," Mrs. Moran told them before leading them to the buses.

Becky climbed on the bus and sat beside Judy. "I'll miss Mrs. Moran. I wonder which teacher we'll have in third-grade?"

Judy shrugged her shoulder. "Do you have to go to summer school?"

"No," Becky shook her head. "But I wish I could. Summer school kids get to go swimming in the morning before the pool opens for the day."

"I forgot about that," Judy said. "Now I wish I had to go to summer school, too."

The line of buses took off heading for the high school to pick up the older kids. The noise level rose as the bus filled with kids.

"Don't get Blake riled up today, J.R.," Becky heard Kurt talking from the seat behind her. "If we have to stop while he makes you get a willow switch, we'll never get home! I want to ride my motorcycle today."

"I'll try," J.R. promised, grinning. "I'll ride mine out to your place when I get home."

"I just built a ramp for the track behind Mom's garden spot," Kurt continued.

Becky tuned out the older boys' conversation. The bus was coming to a stop by the Tastee Freeze. She loved this last day of school tradition.

Their bus driver, Blake, stopped the bus and opened the door. "Everyone off! Let's get some ice cream!"

Bus after bus pulled up around them. The kids poured off the buses and formed lines. There were so many kids! Mrs. Gooding was doing a wonderful job serving ice cream cones as fast as she could. The Gooding girls got off one of the buses and went inside to help their mom serve.

"Thank you," Becky accepted her cone and moved to the side. Shari came to stand beside her, licking the ice cream as it melted.

"We won't see each other again for a long time," Shari said sadly.

"Sure, we will," Beck assured her friend. "There's the parade, the pool, the swimming lessons," she repeated what she had told Sivi.

"I guess," Shari said, catching another drip of ice cream with her tongue. "We can spend the night at each other's houses, too."

They looked up at the sound of a car horn. A car filled with boys was passing by the Tastee Freeze. One boy leaned out the rear window and threw a water balloon. It exploded against a bus tire. The boys laughed and sped away.

Blake took off the engineer cap he always wore and shook it at the boys. "You hooligans. I outta..." He smacked the cap against his leg and put it back on his head. Blake was a pretty easy-going guy, but he expected the kids to behave or else!

They finished their treat and boarded the bus for the trip home.

"I wish I could stay in town for the water balloon fights," J.R. told Kurt.

"You would," Gwen, Kurt's sister, said. "Then you would be getting in trouble along with those older boys, and Blake would be mad at you!"

"Nothing new there," J.R. grinned. He stood up and walked to the front of the bus.

Becky and Judy watched him take his usual place standing on the step. So far, it seemed they would get home without J.R. getting in trouble. When he stood on the step, he usually just opened the door for the kids to get off at their stop. He rarely made Blake mad unless he rode in the back of the bus. J.R. was a good kid, but his nature was to be ornery. He loved to rile people just to see their reaction, especially Blake.

Becky should know. Their dads were best friends. Becky was at the Wilson house all the time, so she knew J.R. pretty well.

This bus ran the Nettleton route. Only a handful of kids lived in Nettleton, their little two-block community. The rest of the kids lived in the country between Hamilton and Nettleton or somewhere around Nettleton. The town school kids were Becky, her little sister Jill and the Wilson kids- J.R., Jason, and Michelle. The Blakelys lived in Nettleton, too, but their kids rode a different bus route with their dad. He was also a bus driver.

The bus was more than half empty when Becky and Jill got off at their trailer house.

"Is Dad going to be home tonight?" Jill asked.

"I don't know," Becky dropped her bag inside the living room door.

Jill threw her bag on top of Becky's.

"Hey!" Becky grabbed her bag. "You're going to crush my sailboat I made in art class."

"I didn't hurt your sailboat."

"You did," Becky insisted. "It's probably flat now."

"So?" Jill stuck her chin in the air. "It's only paper. It won't float anyway!"

"Not now," Becky yelled. "You crushed it!"

"It's paper," Jill yelled back. "When it gets wet, it will fall apart."

"Why would it get wet?"

"It will in the bathtub!"

"I'll put it on the shelf!"

"Girls, stop!" Their mom, Judy, came from the back of the trailer putting an end to their fight before it could escalate in its usual fashion. Sisters only a year and a half apart in age could be very close. They could also be fierce opponents. "Take your bags to your room."

The girls grabbed their bags and headed to the bedroom they shared.

"Becky, be sure to feed Muffin before you go outside to play."

"I will," Becky called from the bedroom.

Muffin is Becky's hamster. When their class hamster had babies, Mrs. Moran had let a few of the students take a baby hamster home. Becky had brought her hamster home last week. She named her Muffin. She is about five weeks old.

"Mom, will Daddy be home tonight?" Jill asked. Their dad, Earl, is an over-the-road truck driver, so he isn't home every night.

"Yes, in about an hour," Mom answered.

"I'm going to check on the baby," Becky told her mom.

"Me, too," Jill followed her sister to the kitchen to grab a snack to eat on the way to the Wilson's.

"Becky, Betty is not going to have the baby for a few more weeks," her mom told her again, for maybe the twentieth time.

"I'm still going to check on him," Becky insisted, one hand on the doorknob, the other holding an apple.

"How do you know it's a boy?"

"I don't know," Becky shrugged her shoulder. "It doesn't seem right to keep calling the baby It."

"That does sound better. Be home in time for supper."

"We will."

Chapter Two

Becky's Latest Obsession

The Wilson house was a block away. They could go the long way or the shortcut. The long way was down the driveway to the gravel road, walk east until the end of the block by Clarkson's store, then turn south until almost the end of the block and cross the street. The shortcut was out the back door heading south, past their mom's beauty salon, then turning east to follow Shaney's fence row and cutting straight across Orie's yard. The Wilson's house was on the other side of the street. Becky decided to ride her bike on the gravel rather than walk through the tall grass by Shaney's fence. Jill rode her bicycle beside Becky down the gravel road.

Becky and Jill played with all the Wilson kids, but mostly Michelle. Their place was like a second home. J.R. was two years older than Becky, Jason was the same age as Becky and Michelle was a year younger than Becky; the same age as Jill. Their mom, Betty, was eight-months pregnant. Becky couldn't hardly wait for the new baby to be born.

Michelle was outside getting on her bike.

"Where are you going, Michelle?" Becky coasted into the yard and pushed down her kickstand.

"I was going to your house."

"Let's ride to my grandma's," Jill suggested.

"You two go ahead," Becky waved them off. "I'm going to see Betty."

"She's still pregnant," Michelle called as they rode away.

Becky ignored her, opening the door to their house. She plowed right into Jason.

"Watch it!" he jumped back.

Becky saw what he was holding. "When did you get a skateboard?"

Jason held out his new blue skateboard. "Mom ordered them a couple of weeks ago. She picked them up today."

"I like it," Becky said.

"I'm going to try it out on the patio." Jason walked around Becky. "Do you want to use J.R.'s or Michelle's? They got one, too."

Becky did want to ride the skateboard, but she wanted to know about the baby even more.

"Not right now."

Jason shrugged and went outside.

Their mom was in the back room doing laundry. They still called it the back porch, even though it had been closed in years ago and was really a room.

Betty turned from the washing machine when she heard Becky enter the room.

"Oh, you are still pregnant," Becky commented, disappointed.

"Now Becky," Betty put her hand on Becky's shoulder. "We talked about this. I will let you know when I have the baby. It'll be a few more weeks."

"I know. That's what Mom said. But a few weeks is a long time!" she complained.

Betty laughed. "Tell me about it!" She rubbed her lower back. "Go play. The baby won't come today."

Becky went back outside. She could see Jason across the road in front of Alborn's big brick building. Most people just called it The Clubhouse. Years ago, it had been a feed store, but now the building was used for meetings and parties.

Jason was trying to ride his skateboard in circles on the little concrete area in front of The Clubhouse. A skateboard would be so much fun. When her dad got home, she would ask him if she could have a skateboard, too.

Becky rode her bicycle to her grandparent's house a block west. She found Jill and Michelle outside her grandpa's garage playing with the dogs. When her dog, Collie, saw her, he ran over and almost knocked Becky off the bike with his enthusiasm.

"Good boy," Becky crooned, rubbing Collie's neck. "Did you miss me?"

Collie licked Becky's cheek.

"Hi, Grandpa," Becky called. His big garage door was open with a car parked inside. She could see his legs sticking out from under the car.

He rolled the creeper out far enough to raise his head. "Done with another year of school, are you?"

"All done and ready for summer!" Becky told him.

Jill walked over carrying Suzie, Red's dog. Suzie squirmed and jumped out of Jill's arms, taking off after a rabbit. Collie ran off with Suzie.

"Come on." Michelle followed the dogs.

"Talk to you later, Grandpa." Becky and Jill ran to catch up with Michelle and the dogs.

When the girls went home later, they saw their dad's baby blue pick-up truck in the driveway.

"Daddy's home!" Jill rushed inside.

Their dad was sitting on the floor with all colors of plastic pieces laying around him.

Earl moved his toothpick to the side of his mouth. "Look in Muffin's cage," Dad told them.

"Oh, wow," Becky sank to her knees in front of the cage. "We have another hamster. Look at him go!" The new hamster was running the wheel, making it spin faster than Muffin ever had.

Jill sat down beside Becky. "Look at Muffin. Do you think she's scared of her new roommate?"

Muffin was huddled in the corner of the cage nibbling on a chunk of carrot.

Their mom came in the room. "He probably intimidates Muffin. She's not used to sharing her cage."

"Which is why I bought this." Earl attached a tube to Muffin's cage, then a bubble to the other end of the tube. "This will give them more room to run."

Becky watched as her dad added more and more pieces to Muffin's cage. Her mom went back to the kitchen to finish preparing supper.

"I'm going to call him Speedy," Becky told her dad, "because he runs really fast."

"It's my turn to name a hamster," Jill protested. "You named Muffin."

"Yeah," Becky told her sister. "Because my teacher gave her to me so she's mine."

"Then Speedy is mine," Jill said.

"See," Becky grinned. "You said Speedy, so that's his name."

"No, it's not," Jill fired back.

"Is so!" Becky argued. "I said Speedy, then you said Speedy. His name is Speedy! And besides, you have your fish. I have hamsters, you have fish."

"Girls! Stop!" Earl snapped the last piece of the cage in place. "We'll call him Speedy. No more arguing. How do you like Muffin's and Speedy's new cage?"

"Wow," they both said. While they were watching Speedy and fighting over his name, their dad had been busy. The cage sprawled all around the television set, on both sides and across the top. The two hamsters were already running through the tunnels.

"I think they like it," Becky said.

"Supper is ready." Mom appeared at the swinging doors that separated the living room and the kitchen. "Earl! What on Earth?"

"Ah, now, Judy..." Earl looked at the girls. "The girls like it."

On cue, both girls nodded.

"But all around the television? Seriously?" Judy kept following the cage with her eyes.

"Please, Mom," Becky begged. "It looks good right where it is."

"Let's just eat," she ushered the girls into the kitchen, but stopped Earl in the doorway. "You, I will talk to later!"

Over supper, Becky told her dad about Jason's new skateboard.

"A skateboard would be so much fun, Daddy," Becky gushed. "You can turn this way and that way. You can go in circles in both directions. Even do figure eights. You can do tricks with them, too. Can I have one, please? Pretty please?"

"Now, Becky," Earl began.

"J.R. and Michelle have one, too," Becky added. "They didn't even play with theirs and they are brand new. Michelle rode bikes and played with the dogs with me and Jill. J.R. rode his motorcycle out to Kurt's house."

"I don't think a skateboard is a good idea," Earl laid down his fork and gave Becky his full attention. "You could get hurt. A skateboard can be dangerous. You've watched them wreck skateboards on television."

"I've watched them have fun and do stunts and tricks on television," Becky corrected him. She pouted. "But Michelle has one!"

"Becky," her mom warned. Their parents had explained to them many times that just because Michelle has something, doesn't mean they will always get the same thing. Becky had heard Betty say the same thing, visa versa, to Michelle.

"Fine!" Becky crossed her arms. "I'll just watch my friends have all the fun!"

Chapter Three

Smokey, Big and Tall

Becky was still pouting about the skateboard on Monday. She did get to sleep late over the weekend, but today her mom had woken her up early for swimming and riding lessons. Riding lessons were one of the presents they had received last Christmas. Today was their first lesson. Because Judy's salon was open Tuesday through Saturday, lessons were to be on Monday's in Cameron, a town about twenty miles west of Nettleton.

Swimming lessons began at 9:00 a.m. Riding lessons were at 11:00 a.m.

"Girls," Judy, standing between the two girls, put an arm around each of them. "This is Sue. She is your riding instructor."

"Hello." Sue took off her gloves and stuck them in her back pocket. "You must be Becky and Jill?"

They nodded.

"Would you like to meet Smokey?"

They nodded again.

"He's beautiful." Jill reached out to stroke his belly. "He's so tall."

Becky stayed beside Mom, not sure about getting close to such a big, tall horse. She was expected to ride *him?*

"This is Smokey," Sue introduced them to the horse, stroking his mane. She led Becky to the horse, away from her mom. Becky slowly reached up to pet Smokey.

"Who wants to go first?"

"Me!" Jill raised her hand immediately.

Becky took a deep breath. Of course, Jill wanted to go first. She was fearless. Becky was not going to be out done by her little sister. "I will," she said firmly. *If Jill can do it, I can do it.*

Sue led Smokey to a mounting block. Becky knew how to mount a horse. They had a couple of horses when the girls were little, but they had to sell them because they kept getting out of the electric fence and roaming all over Nettleton.

Smokey fidgeted when Becky settled in the saddle. She leaned down and hugged Smokey's neck, clenching her legs tight on either side of his back.

"Calm down, Becky." Sue patted Becky's leg with one hand and smoothed Smokey's rump with the other. "The two of you will soon be good friends. I'm going to adjust the straps, then we will walk around the corral while you and Smokey get to know each other."

Becky was nervous when the horse started walking. She felt her body tilt to one side, then tilt to the other side.

After several turns around the corral, Sue stopped and held out Smokey's reins. "Are you ready to try this by yourself?"

"I think so," Becky took a deep breath getting up her courage.

"Just click your heels and snap the reins," Sue instructed.

Click my heels, Becky couched herself silently. *Not too hard, Smokey might run.*

Becky's heels touched the horse's flanks, but Smokey didn't move.

"A little harder." Sue was so patient.

Becky tried again.

"You can do it, Becky. One more time."

This time Becky clicked a little too hard. Smokey didn't take off at a run, but he did take off fast enough to make Becky jerk back in the saddle. She sat back up straight right away.

She did it! Smokey was walking without Sue's help. Becky reached forward to pat Smokey's neck. "Good boy."

Smokey stopped. *Uh, oh!* Now Becky had to get him started again. She clicked her tongue and shook the reins. Darn it. She was going to have to click her heels, too. She tried again. Yes! Smokey moved. She didn't even jerk, just made Becky's body shift as she walked.

Her mom and Jill were leaning against the fence watching Becky walk the horse. As Becky passed them, she grinned.

"I did it, Mom," she said. "Did you see me? I got Smokey started two times!"

"You are doing wonderful," Mom encouraged.

"Alright, Becky. Bring Smokey over to the mounting block," Sue motioned with her hand.

Sue grabbed Smokey's reins to help Becky stop the horse, then helped her dismount.

"Did you like riding by yourself?"

"It was great!" Becky couldn't stop smiling.

"Now we are going to learn how to sit properly. I want you to squat down and pretend you are sitting on Smokey."

That was easy. She had been sitting on Smokey long enough, even standing on the ground it felt like her legs were still around his back. Becky followed her instructions. Sue put one hand on Becky's lower back and the other on her shoulder.

"Now move your shoulders back. You should be in a straight line from your ear, shoulder, hip and heel."

"This feels weird," Becky giggled.

"If you lean forward, your heels push back," Sue explained. "If you lean back, your heels shoot forward. That could confuse Smokey, or even make you fall to the ground if he took off running. You have more control if you sit straight."

"Okay," Becky concentrated on remembering this position. She did not want to fall off Smokey. It was a long way to the ground when you were sitting in that saddle. "Ear, shoulder, hip and heel. Got it."

"Now let's talk about the proper way to mount Smokey."

Becky learned a lot during her first riding lesson. She paid attention when it was Jill's turn, also.

On the way home she told her mom, "I can't wait until the next lesson!"

"Me, either," Jill said. "I love Smokey. Mom, when can we get our own horse?"

"Your father and I explained that when we told you about the lessons. When Sue thinks you are ready, we will get you a horse."

"Can we keep him in the side yard like we did with the other horses we had before?" Becky asked.

"No," Mom shook her head. "I'm not chasing them all over Nettleton again. We'll have to find a place to board your horse when the time comes."

Chapter Four

Lunch at Clarkson's Store

Becky checked on Betty's baby every day that week.

"Are you excited about the baby?" Becky asked Michelle while they played Barbie's.

"Of course," Michelle put Skipper in the elevator of the townhouse. "I hope Mom has a boy. I don't want to share my room."

"I like your new room," Becky said, while she buttoned her Barbie's dress.

Michelle had been sharing a bedroom with her brothers until recently. Her parents had this room built onto the house just for her.

"I like the matching bedspread and curtains," Jill said. She sat her Barbie on the couch of the townhouse.

Betty had decorated Michelle's bedroom in pink with green and white accents. There was a lot of pink! Becky loved the way Betty coordinated everything in a room. The living room was browns, oranges and yellows. She liked the fancy orange recliners. Someday she would decorate her own house, and all her stuff would match, too.

"Let's go to Clarkson's for lunch," Becky suggested. "I'll get some money from Mom and meet you at the store." The Wilson's had a charge account at the store, but Becky and Jill always went home to get money. Not long ago, the Wilson kids had run the bill up to $200. Betty had been mad, mad, mad. Michelle had told Becky and Jill all about how much trouble they had gotten into. Now Becky understood why her mom and dad liked to pay as they went.

Michelle grabbed her skateboard. "Do you want to use J.R.'s and Jason's skateboards? We can ride to the store."

"We can't," Becky told her. "Daddy says they are dangerous."

"I haven't wrecked mine," Michelle pointed out. "I ride it on the patio. Last night, J.R. was riding his from the back porch by the washing machine, through the kitchen and dining room to the front door. He didn't stop fast enough and the pointy front on his skateboard went through the door. Come on, I'll show you," she put her skateboard back in closet.

Becky and Jill followed her through the living room. Michelle pointed at the hole about three inches from the bottom of the door. It was about half an inch tall and maybe four inches wide. "Mom didn't even yell at him!"

"Your mom is so neat," Becky told Michelle. "Like when she let us move the furniture out of the way in the living room and roller skate. Remember, it was in January, a couple of weeks after my birthday? It was snowing so bad they wouldn't let us go to The Country Place, so Betty let us make our own skating rink inside."

"That was fun," Jill said. "The wooden floor was really noisy, too, with all of us skating at the same time."

"When I grow up," Becky said, "I'm going to have a lot of kids and I'm going to be a neat mom just like Betty. I'm going to let my kids have fun and not yell at them for every little thing."

"I like my mom," Michelle agreed. "Your dad is funny, too."

"I hope Daddy doesn't hear about this," Becky said, pointing at the hole in the door. "It will be another reason he won't allow me to get a skateboard."

"I want one, too," Jill said. "I didn't at first, but now I do."

"You want me to have my dad talk to your dad?" Michelle offered. "That works sometimes."

"First let me ask him again when he comes home next," Becky told her friend.

"I think my dad will be home this week, too," Michelle told them. Leon is a trucker, just like Earl, but he hauls permit loads, which means he can only drive from dawn to dusk, so his loads take longer to deliver.

"Let's go," Jill pushed them out the door. "I'm hungry."

Becky met them at Nathan and Frances Clarkson's store. Nathan was already cutting bologna for their sandwiches. They pulled a pop out of the old coke machine, then used the opener to take off the cap. Becky and Jill chose Dr. Pepper, and Michelle got a R.C. Cola.

Becky angled her head to see how many caps were in the bottle cap holder. "It's getting full, Michelle. You'll have to empty it soon." Frances let Michelle take the bottle caps for her collection.

"Already?" Michelle leaned over to look. "I just emptied it not long ago!"

"What are your plans for today?" Frances asked when they stepped to the counter. She rang up Becky's and Jill's food, then wrote Michelle's in her ledger.

"I'm not sure what we'll do next," Becky told her as she passed Frances the money she'd gotten from her mom.

"We played Barbies this morning," Jill told Frances.

"Bring your bottles back in when you're done, and I'll let you pick out a candy bar."

"We will," Michelle promised.

They sat on the front step of the store to eat their lunch.

"How about if our Barbies go camping after we eat?" Jill suggested.

"That sounds like fun," Michelle agreed.

"They could camp under the big tree by Bimbo's dog house," Becky added, referring to her dad's dog.

Michelle took a drink of her R.C. "Here comes J.R. on his skateboard. Mine and Jason's are just one color, but his is neat. Have you seen it yet?"

Becky and Jill shook their heads as J.R. rolled to a stop. He stomped on the back of the board, and it flipped up so he could grab it.

"Quit showing off," Michelle told her big brother.

"I like your skateboard," Becky told J.R.

J.R. turned it over so they could see it better. It had a beach design with the sun and palm trees on it in green, orange, yellow and red. "Mine is the best. I used a screwdriver to adjust the wheels."

"Why?" Becky wanted to know.

J.R. put the skateboard back on the sidewalk and stood on it. He shifted his weight from one side to the other. "See how it tilts? Now I can turn easier. I'll show you." He rode the skateboard to the end of the sidewalk, turned around by leaning to the left, then came back towards them, weaving from one side of the wide sidewalk to the other.

"See," J.R. said. "I have better control."

"I want a skateboard so bad," Becky sighed.

J.R. pushed Becky's and Michelle's shoulders farther apart and stepped between them to go into the store, leaving his skateboard on the sidewalk. Becky stared at it as she ate the last of her sandwich.

She could picture herself riding it, going faster and faster, turning in circles.

A car stopped in the parking area. Mary and her daughter, Linda, got out and crossed the gravel to the sidewalk.

"Hello, girls," Mary greeted them. "It's another muggy day, isn't it?"

They nodded and moved off the step so Mary could enter the store. Linda stayed outside. Linda is the same age as Jill and Michelle.

"Did you hear? The Blakely's are moving. They are taking their trailer with them," Linda said.

"They are moving the whole trailer?" Jill asked. "Really?"

"Yeah. They are going to build a house, so they are moving the trailer to the land they bought on the other side of Hamilton. They plan to stay in the trailer while they build the new house," Linda explained.

"That must be why we haven't see them lately," Becky said.

They moved to the end of the building to look at Blakely's trailer across the road. "It'll look funny without the trailer there," Michelle said.

The Blakelys have three kids, but they were never home. "They must be working late every night on building the new house. That's why they aren't ever home," Linda said.

"Hey, you want to play Barbies with us?" Jill asked Linda. "We are taking them camping in our back yard."

Linda shook her head. "I can't. We have to pick John up in Hamilton. Mom just wanted to get the mail out of our post office box."

They heard a loud noise and turned in time to see a black semi-truck come up the hill and over the railroad tracks.

"My dad's home," Michelle said. "I didn't know he was coming home today!"

J.R. must have heard the semi-truck from inside the store. He came out with a Coke bottle in his hand and took off down the gravel road carrying his skateboard.

"I'm going to see my dad," Michelle told them.

"What about your candy bar?" Becky asked, which reminded Michelle she had promised Frances they would all return the empty bottles.

"Can you give this to Frances for me?" She held out her empty R.C. bottle.

Jill took it. "We'll bring you a Chunky candy bar, okay?"

"Thanks." Michelle ran down the sidewalk in front of Blakely's trailer, past Shaney's house, and down Orie's driveway, then across the road.

Mary came out of the store and Linda had to leave.

"I should go see if Betty's ready to have the baby," Becky told her sister.

"We were just there before lunch," Jill reminded her. "I'm pretty sure she is still pregnant."

Becky took Michelle's R.C. bottle from Jill. "Let's give these to Frances. We'll take Michelle her candy bar."

Becky grabbed a solid chocolate Chunky for Michelle and M & M's for herself. Jill got her favorite, a Snicker's Bar.

"Was that Leon I heard down the road?"

The girls turned around to see who was talking to them. Several men were sitting around the unlit wood stove. Clarkson's was where the men came to sit around and talk. There were several mismatched chairs for them to use. Today the men were Joe, Orie and Ralph.

"Yes," Becky said. "He just got home."

"Tell him to come by my place later." Joe was the man talking to them.

"We will," they promised.

That Evel Knievel Wanna Be

Chapter Five

The screen door banged shut behind them as they took off running down the sidewalk. They reached Michelle's house the same time as Jason. He rode his dirt bike into the yard. The girls sprinted for the front porch. Jason had chased them with his dirt bike a few times. He wasn't mean, just ornery like his older brother.

"Want a ride?" Jason twisted the handle, revving the engine.

"I do," Becky yelled over the noise.

"I'll give Leon Joe's message." Jill disappeared into the house.

Becky climbed on the dirt bike behind Jason. As usual, he took off at practically full throttle. He drove across the road to his Grandpa Manley's and Grandma Helen's house and into their back yard. They went between the two rows of sheds to the very back of the property where J.R. and Jason had circled the old vehicles so many times they had a dirt track. After a few laps, they crossed the railroad tracks to Gardner's logging property. He stopped just shy of the loading dock.

"Don't you dare jump that ramp with me on here!" Becky yelled in his ear.

"Come on," Jason revved the engine again. "Don't be a chicken. I'm getting better."

"Let me off. I'll watch," Becky insisted.

"Never mind," Jason told her. "I'll jump it later." They took off again. "Wanna pop a wheelie?"

"No!" Becky yelled back. "I'll fall off! Take me back to your house."

Jason let her off by the patio, then rode back down to the tracks. He spun the dirt bike around in a circle, pivoting on the front wheel, then came back down the road, shifting hard. He popped a wheelie right in front of the house. He turned around by Shaney's garage and came back to where Becky stood watching him.

"Pretty good, huh?" he grinned.

"You're getting better," Becky told him, "but you still only raised the front wheel this much." She spread her hands about a foot apart.

Jason stuck out his tongue and roared off, spraying dirt behind him.

Jill and Michelle came outside. "What is Jason doing now?"

"He's practicing popping wheelies," Becky told them. "That boy has been watching too much Evel Knievel!"

When Becky's dad came home later that week, she once again asked him for a skateboard.

"Beck," Daddy said, "skateboards can be dangerous. What if you fell and got hurt?"

"How can I get hurt, Daddy?" Becky argued. She held up both hands a few inches apart. "They are only this tall. J.R. fixed his skateboard. He can have a lot of fun. He's really good on his board."

"I'll think about it," her dad compromised.

"I want one, too, Daddy," Jill climbed on his lap. "We both need a skateboard."

"I said I will think about it, but for now the answer is no." He pulled a toothpick out of the holder and put it in his mouth, signaling the end of the conversation.

Becky laid on the floor to watch her hamsters. Speedy was spinning the wheel as fast as his little legs could run.

If I had a skateboard, Becky thought, *I could ride it as fast as Speedy runs his wheel.*

The next morning Becky went across the street to see her Grandma. She picked up the Raggedy Ann doll and flopped down on the couch.

"What's wrong, Becky?" Grandma asked.

"I can't talk Daddy into letting me have a skateboard," Becky pouted.

"Did he tell you why you couldn't have one?"

"He thinks I'll get hurt," she hugged Raggedy Ann.

"You know your Daddy loves you," Grandma reminded Becky. "He would never want anything bad to happen to you."

"Michelle's had her skateboard for over a week and she hasn't gotten hurt!"

"Everyone is different. I'm glad Michelle hasn't been hurt, but that doesn't mean you couldn't get hurt."

"I suppose," Becky mumbled. "I would promise to be careful." Becky was quiet for a minute. "I asked Daddy again last night."

"And what did he say?" Grandma raised one eyebrow, waiting.

"He said he'd think about it."

"Well, there you go. Let's give him a few days to think about it, okay?"

"I guess," Becky nodded, knowing she didn't have any other choice except to wait for her dad to decide.

"Would you like a cookie and some Kool-Aid?"

Becky followed her grandma to the kitchen.

Chapter Six

Rice Krispie Treats & Tetherball

Tuesday was their second day of swim lessons. Becky was excited. Her and Jill were riding to Hamilton with the Wilson's, but after swim lessons were over, Becky was walking home with one of her best friends, Shari, to spend the night.

Becky stood next to Shari on the edge of the pool, waiting for the lifeguard to blow the whistle.

"I like swim lessons," she told Shari, "but I dread getting in the water."

"Oh, I know." Shari understood completely. "The water was freezing cold yesterday."

"It was so cold, I'm glad I didn't have to go to summer school."

"Me, too," Shari nodded. "I think the bus brings them here as soon as our lesson is over."

Brrr. The whistle blew. Becky was trying to decide whether to stick her toe in to see how cold the water really was, or just jump in. The decision was made for her when J.R. walked behind her and shoved her back. *SPLASH!*

Becky's head popped out of the water, her red hair dripping. She opened her mouth to yell at him, but he was already down by the pit, walking backwards. He pointed at Becky, laughing.

Shari bobbed toward her in the water. She had jumped in before J.R. could push her in, too. "I tell you- *boys!*" Shari knows exactly how ornery boys could be; she has four older brothers.

"He's always picking on me!" Becky said.

"Tell me about it." Shari rolled her eyes. "He's just getting you ready to deal with my brothers tonight."

"I'm ready," Becky grinned, then shivered. "I'm cold, too."

"Line up," Jan, the lifeguard, blew the whistle.

Becky could see Jill on the other side of the pool with a bunch of her friends. Jill was in a different swimming lesson class.

Swimming lessons were mostly given in the three-foot area of the pool for the younger kids. As they progressed, the class would move to deeper water.

"Hold on to the side and let's see everyone blow bubbles."

Becky dutifully blew bubbles. Next the instructor had them practice scissor kicking with their legs. Another lifeguard pulled them aside two at a time to use the paddle boards.

After swim lessons, Becky ran to Betty's car to get her overnight case.

"Please don't have the baby until I get home," Becky begged Betty.

"I'm not going to have the baby tonight," Betty laughed. "You have a fun time at Shari's. I'll see you here at the pool in the morning."

Becky ran over to where Shari was waiting with her brothers. "I'm ready."

The two girls half-walked, half-ran to keep up with the boys. They stopped several times on the route home to check the fruit trees and vines growing in people's yards. The plum tree was still blooming. The apple tree in Hartley's yard wasn't ready, either.

Jeff, Shari's brother, popped a grape in his mouth. "Not ready, yet," he told them. "Later this summer we'll have plenty to snack on all the way home."

At Shari's house, they followed her brothers into the kitchen. Shari's mom had left all the ingredients for rice krispie treats on the kitchen table.

"Where is your mom?" Becky asked, eating a marshmallow.

"She left a note." David walked to the fridge and pulled the paper from under a magnet. "I have Heather with me. Went to Aunt Ruth's house. Be back before supper," he read out loud.

Heather is Shari, Dennis, Brad, Jeff, and David's little sister.

Dennis grabbed the bag of marshmallows from Shari. "Don't eat all of them. Go outside. We'll make the rice krispie treats. They will need to set in the fridge for at least half an hour."

"Okay, but save some rice krispie treats for us." Shari picked up her jump rope. Becky followed her outside.

"Here, Becky, you go first," Shari handed her the rope.

Becky was looking at the tree in the front yard. "Let's tie it to that branch and turn it into a swing." She pointed to a low branch.

"You want to climb the tree, or should I?"

"You go ahead," Becky said. "I'll throw the rope up to you."

Shari climbed the boards her brothers had nailed to the tree to use as a ladder. When she reached the branch, she scooted out about halfway.

"Hey, Becky," Shari called down. "Come up here. There's a bird's nest with babies in it."

Becky scurried up the tree.

"Oh," Becky crooned, "they are so little!"

"Maybe we should feed them," Shari said. "They sound hungry."

The girls climbed back down the tree and headed for the ditch.

"This is where my brothers get worms for fishing," Shari told Becky. "Try looking under rocks."

Becky found a stick and started poking it in the mud.

"What are you doing?" Brad hollered from the front porch. He walked over to where they were crouching by the ditch. Dennis walked over with him.

"We need to find worms to feed the baby birds," Becky told him. "They chirp like they are starving."

Dennis laughed. "You can't feed them worms like that."

"Why not?" Shari demanded. "All birds like worms."

"New birds eat food their parents chew up for them," Dennis explained.

"You mean the mom chews the food, then takes it out of her mouth and puts it in the baby's mouth?"

Dennis nodded.

"Yuck. That's gross," Becky said.

"I'm not chewing a worm for them," Shari stated.

"Me, either," Becky grimaced.

"Don't worry about the baby birds. The momma bird is probably getting food for them now if she's not in the nest." Dennis and Brad took off down the road.

"Well, now what?" Shari looked around. "There's Neil." She pointed to one of their classmates across the street in his backyard. "Let's get the rice krispie treats. We'll take Neil one, too."

The girls rushed inside and grabbed the pan out of the fridge. Shari was holding the knife when Jeff walked into the kitchen.

"They are probably still soft and gooey," he pointed out.

"We're hungry now," Becky told him.

Jeff shrugged his shoulders. "They'll taste the same. Cut me one, too," he told Shari.

They grabbed their snack and ran back outside and across the street.

"Thanks," Neil told the girls when they gave him the rice krispie treat.

The trio sat on the back step of Neil's house while they ate. When they were done, Neil turned on the water hose. They took turns rinsing their sticky hands and getting a drink.

"Ready to play tetherball?" Neil asked.

They each chose a spot to stand around the pole.

Neil hit the ball as hard as he could. Becky and Shari stuck out their hands, trying to stop the ball, but around and around the pole it went.

"I'm almost glad I missed," Becky said. "That one might have hurt."

Becky served the ball next, but Neil stopped it.

On Shari's turn, the ball wrapped around the pole.

Shari and Neil had both scored. Becky hadn't. Becky was determined to hit that ball hard on her next turn. She swung her hand back for momentum, then aimed for the ball. She missed the ball, but her arm swung her body in a circle and she lost her balance, falling to the ground.

Neil laughed.

Becky stood up and brushed the dirt off her shorts. She'd show Neil! Not only was she going to hit that ball; it was going to fly right past Neil so he couldn't stop it.

With her jaw set, Becky smacked the ball. *Yes!* Around and around it went, right past Neil's and Shari's hands. She was in the game!

The girls played in Neil's yard until they saw Shari's dad's pick-up pull in their driveway. They ran across the road.

Chapter Seven

Lightening Bugs and Dandelions

"Hi, Daddy," Shari said.

"Hi, Lefty," Becky greeted him. Shari's dad was missing part of one arm, so everyone called him Lefty.

They started to follow him into the kitchen, but Shari saw the bag of squirrels he was trying to hide behind his back, so she turned to climb the stairs instead. If Becky knew they were having fried squirrel for supper, she might not eat. Which meant Shari's mom would have gathered onions, zucchini and tomatoes from the garden for supper as well. *Yum!*

In Shari's bedroom, they got the Barbie's out and sat cross-legged on the bed.

"Let's dress them for the beach," Becky told Shari. "They can go surfing."

"What have you been doing since school got out for the summer?" Shari asked.

"Well, me and Jill started riding lessons," Becky said. "I was really nervous. Sue's horse Smokey is tall. But after my lesson yesterday, I'm not nervous anymore."

"I love horses," Shari said. "When I grow up, I'm always going to own horses."

"Daddy brought home another hamster, and he built this big hamster cage. The cage goes all around the television set now."

"Wow," said Shari.

"Yeah," Becky brushed the Barbie's hair. "I asked him if I could have a skateboard."

"What did he say?"

"He said no the first time I asked. I asked him again and now he is thinking about it," Becky said glumly.

"Cheer up," Shari told her. "Usually if he's thinking about it, he's going to say 'yes' the next time."

"I hope you're right. What I really hope is for Jason's mom to have her baby," Becky's mood lifted. "But not tonight!"

"I forgot she was going to have another baby," Shari said.

"She promised me she wouldn't have it tonight while I'm not home."

Heather, Shari's little sister, came in the room. That meant Shari's mom was home and probably fixing supper.

"Mom says for you to feed the bunnies," Heather told Shari.

"Okay." The girls left the Barbies on the bed and went outside, Heather trailing behind them.

Behind the house, Jeff was feeding the dog. Shari led the way to the bunnies' cage.

"Look at her babies," Shari told Becky.

"Ah, how cute." Becky picked one up to cuddle.

"That's Sugar," Heather told Becky. Heather picked up a bunny with darker fur. "This is Fluffy. She's my favorite." Heather rubbed her cheek against Fluffy's head.

"How many babies did she have?" Becky tried to count them but they kept hopping around.

"She had eight, but one disappeared," Shari answered.

"A fox probably got it," Jeff told them.

"That's so mean," Shari told her brother. "Maybe he hopped away and is living in the country."

"Hopefully," Becky agreed.

"Supper!" Shari's mom yelled out the back door.

When they went inside, Carol was pulling the big cast iron skillet out of the oven. She had fried the squirrel and smothered it in salsa.

"This is good," Becky said, chewing a bite of the meat.

"That's squi-, hey!" Shari had kicked David under the table before he could tell Becky she was eating squirrel. "That is good, huh?" he snickered.

"It's my favorite," Shari told Becky. "Becky, do you want to sleep outside tonight? We could make a tent."

Becky nodded.

"I want to sleep outside, too," Heather said.

Carol patted Heather's hand. "I think you better stay inside with me and the guys."

"No," Heather smacked the table. "I'm staying outside with the girls."

"That's enough," Lefty said, his tone letting Heather know better than to argue.

Heather crossed her arms and stuck out her lower lip.

Becky wanted to tell her she could sleep outside with them, but it really would be more fun with just herself and Shari.

"You can sleep outside with us next time," Shari compromised.

After supper, the girls started making their tent. They took two chairs from the kitchen table outside.

"Where should we put our tent?" Becky looked over the yard from her vantage point on the front porch.

"Over there," Shari pointed to the side yard. "Under the tree where the grass is tallest. We'll have more cushion to sleep on."

"Good idea," Becky agreed.

They placed the chairs in position, back to back a few feet apart, then went back inside to get some blankets.

"Oh, no. Stop right there," Carol blocked their exit. "You are not taking your Grandma's quilt outside. Use the blankets on the bottom shelf in the closet." She folded the quilt and put it on the back of the couch where the girls had found it.

They tried to arrange the blanket over the chairs, but it kept sliding to the ground.

"I think we need another chair," Becky suggested finally.

"Me, too," Shari nodded. "One on each side and another in the back. We can put our pillows here. Then we'll be able to see the house and the yard and any cars driving by."

They lugged another chair out of the house.

"That'll work," Becky rubbed her hands together, admiring their tent.

"See the lightening bug?" Shari pointed. "Let's catch some and make a bracelet."

They got a canning jar from the kitchen. Heather helped them catch lightening bugs. They ran all over the yard, chasing them until the jar was filled with little flashing lights.

They sat down in a circle in the grass. It didn't take long to pull the lights off the bugs and stick them to their wrists.

Heather held out her arm and spun in circles, watching her glowing arm. "I'm pretty."

Dennis came outside. "Mom says you need to take a bath," he told Heather.

"No," Heather stomped her foot. "I'm staying here!"

Dennis grabbed her around the waist. He carried her into the house under his arm like a sack of potatoes.

"Let's add a dandelion necklace." Becky started picking the yellow weeds.

"We could make crowns, too," Shari said.

When they each had a good sized yellow bouquet, they started weaving the stems together.

"I'm going to enter the princess contest at school next year," Becky told Shari. "I'll wear my prettiest dress and my mom can fix my hair fancy. The winner gets a real princess crown." She placed her dandelion crown on her head.

"I want to enter the princess contest, too," Shari said.

Carol came outside to check on the girls. "Aren't you two of the prettiest girls in town?" She admired their bracelets, necklaces and crowns. "I'm going to bed. Stay in the yard tonight."

"We will," they promised.

The next day at the pool, Becky was relieved to see that Betty hadn't had the baby while she was at Shari's.

Chapter Eight

J.R.-The Handyman

Becky's dad walked into the trailer at the end of the week carrying two matching orange skateboards. Becky hugged him, grinning from ear to ear. "Thank you, thank you, thank you, Daddy. I love it!"

"I want you to be careful," he pointed first at Becky, then at Jill. "I mean it."

"We will," they both promised, struggling to look solemn so he would know they understood how important this was to him. But they couldn't stop smiling.

"I'm going to Michelle's," Becky declared.

"Wait for me," Jill hurried to put on her shoes.

"I'll be over to talk to Leon when he gets home later," Earl called after them.

Jill followed Becky out the back door of the trailer to their mom's salon. A couple of years ago, their dad had rounded up some of his friends and they had built Judy this salon. It resembled a small barn but was painted white with black shutters.

Becky opened the door and ran inside. "Look what Daddy bought us!" She held up her bright orange skateboard.

Judy was rolling a permanent wave on Sylvia, Kurt's mom.

"I see," Judy dutifully admired their new skateboards. "Did you tell your daddy thank you?"

"We did," Jill said.

"We're going to Michelle's house. Bye."

There weren't any sidewalks by Becky's house, but there was one that ran the entire length of the block across from Michelle's house and on both sides of the road from the old hotel to the churches.

Michelle was outside swinging. "Grab your skateboard, Michelle. Look what we got. Let's go ride them." Becky was so excited she couldn't hardly think straight.

Becky walked around the patio, shoving the toys off into the grass with her foot. With the patio emptied, she set down her skateboard. Putting one foot on it, she rolled it back and forth. She rode to one end of the patio. Leaning over, she turned the board around with her hands, then rode back to the other end, meeting Jill going the opposite direction.

Michelle came back outside with her red skateboard. She started riding in circles around the edge of the patio. Becky followed her, until she reached the first corner and could hardly make her board tilt for the turn. She leaned to the side, but her skateboard wouldn't turn as tight as Michelle's did. Jill's wouldn't, either.

Michelle stopped to look at Becky's board. "J.R. had to adjust mine. It wouldn't turn in small circles when I first got it."

"Where is J.R.? I need him to fix mine." Becky looked around the yard. His bicycle was under the tree, and his motorcycle was by the propane tank.

"I think he is talking to Grandpa Manley."

Becky picked up her skateboard and started walking across the street to Michelle's grandparents' house. Jill and Michelle followed, carrying their skateboards, too.

They found J.R. and Manley in the kitchen.

"What is all that?" Becky tried to figure out what they were building.

Manley was sitting at the kitchen table. J.R. was standing beside him. There were little engine parts laying all over the area in front of Manley, who was holding what looked like a weird-shaped metal ball.

"Grandpa is helping me rebuild this carbonator for a go cart," J.R. explained.

"Here," Becky shoved the skateboard into J.R.'s hands. "We need our skateboards fixed. Daddy just gave them to us and they won't turn."

Jill held hers out to J.R., too.

"Michelle," Grandpa Manley said, taking Jill's skateboard, "go in my bedroom and get another screwdriver." She took off. "It's on the table by my bed," he called after her.

J.R. worked on Becky's skateboard while Manley adjusted Jill's. J.R. put it on the floor and tried to skate from the pantry to the bathroom. "It needs

loosened up a little more." He used the screwdriver on it again, then gave it another test run across the kitchen. "That's better." He shoved the board with his foot. It rolled back to Becky.

Manley put Jill's board on the floor. "Give this one a spin, J.R."

Soon the girls were back outside with better working skateboards. "We can go on the sidewalk from here all the way to the store," Becky pointed to the north.

They rode the boards on the short sidewalk from Manley's front door to the edge of his yard. They had to carry them across the gravel road. Then they skated up the sidewalk to the wider concrete area in front of Alborn's brick building. This little area, long ago, was probably the loading dock back when the building used to be a feed store. Here Becky tried to go in circles once again.

"Mine works!" Becky cheered. "Try yours, Jill."

They chased each other for a few laps then continued up the sidewalk. In front of Orie's house, they had to carry their skateboards over a section of tilted and broken sidewalk. They put them back down but had to pick them up again at Orie's driveway. They made it past Shaney's house, but in front of Blakely's trailer there was tufts of grass growing out of the cracks of the sidewalk. Then they had to carry them across another gravel road. Finally, they were at Clarkson's store.

"This is much better," Jill said. "We can ride all the way down this side, around the corner and to the far end."

"It's wide enough for us to race, too," Michelle added.

"Let's have a race now," Becky was excited. "We'll start back here."

The girls lined up on the south end of the building facing the hotel.

"On your mark, get set, go!" Becky called out. They took off. The corner was fun. Becky tried to get up enough speed to ride around the corner like a surfer. She held her arms out for balance.

Jill was trying not to bump into Michelle and ended up going straight instead of turning. She jumped off the board, but the board kept going and stopped in the road. She went after it and picked it up.

"Good thing you jumped," Becky told her. "If you had wrecked and gotten hurt, Daddy might regret giving these to us."

"That wouldn't be good," Michelle shook her head.

"Let's try again," Jill said.

Becky carried her board back to the starting point and took off again. She made it around the corner and all the way down the building. On her way back, the screen door opened and Frances stepped outside.

Becky jumped off her skateboard and it rolled into the concrete wall. "Sorry, Frances."

"You're fine," Frances smiled. "I was wondering what you girls were doing."

"We got new skateboards," Jill told her. "Is it okay if we skate here?"

"It's the smoothest sidewalk," Michelle explained.

"And the widest!" Becky added.

"I don't mind at all," Frances assured them, opening the screen door to go back inside. "Have a good time."

The girls skated back and forth. Becky practiced weaving from one side of the sidewalk to the other like J.R. had done last week.

"I'm getting pretty good at this," Becky called as she passed Michelle.

"There's your dad," Michelle pointed.

Earl parked in the middle of the road between the store and the hotel. He walked to where they were playing in front of the empty end of the building where the bank used to be way back before they were even born.

"How's it going?" He looked them over. "No wrecks? No scrapes?"

"Nope," Becky held her arms out for him to examine, then lifted her legs one at a time to show him her knees weren't even scraped. "All's good."

"Watch this, Daddy." Jill took off on her skateboard, riding around the corner nice and smooth.

Becky and Michelle followed her.

"You're getting the hang of it, aren't you, Poon?" Daddy said when she rolled to a stop in front of him.

Jill nodded.

"I'll pay for a pop and candy bar for each of you while I'm in the store. You can get it when you're ready."

"Thanks, Daddy," they said.

"And we love our skateboards," Becky called after him.

Earl went inside.

"I'm thirsty now," Michelle said. "I want a gold Chunky, too."

Jill nodded.

"Go ahead," Becky told them. "I'm going to practice some more."

Michelle got a Chunky and a R.C. Jill chose a Snickers and a Dr. Pepper. They were sitting on the step eating when Becky rolled to a stop in front of them.

"I've been thinking," Becky sat between them. "We need to have a skateboard club."

"What would we do in the club?" Michelle asked.

"We could have meetings and races," Becky explained. "I'm going to get my candy. I'll be right back." She walked into the store.

Her dad was standing at the counter paying for his car polish. Earl worked hard keeping his vehicles clean.

"I got a call from your grandpa while I was here," Earl said. "He needs us to run to Hamilton to pick up a radiator hose for him at Hamilton Supply."

"But, Daddy, we're riding skateboards," Becky reminded him.

"Load 'em up," Earl said firmly.

"Alright." Becky pulled a bottle of Dr. Pepper out of the coke machine and popped the lid off using the opener. "I'll tell Jill."

She walked outside carrying her drink and M&M's. "We have to go with Daddy to Hamilton," Becky told her sister. "We'll talk to you later about the club," she told Michelle.

Becky didn't get a chance to ride her skateboard again for a few days.

Chapter Nine

"You Can Do It!"

Week two of swim lessons began once again with freezing cold water, followed by riding lessons.

On Tuesday afternoon, while their mom worked, it rained. Becky and Jill stayed in the trailer, watching television.

Michelle walked into Becky and Jill's trailer, folding her umbrella. She was cradling her baby doll in her arms.

"Since we can't ride our skateboards, do you want to play dolls?" she asked.

They went in the bedroom Becky and Jill shared. Jill sat her doll in the highchair. "I'm going to feed Chrissy."

"My baby is hungry, too." Michelle sat on the bed. She stuck a bottle in her doll's mouth. The toy bottle had white liquid in it. The more you tilted the bottle, the emptier it looked. "All done. Time to burp." She held the doll to her shoulder and patted her back.

"We are getting practice for when Betty has the baby," Becky told them.

"My mom said the baby will be heavier than my doll," Michelle said.

"I wonder if your mom's baby will have a lot of hair?" Jill mused.

Becky looked at her doll. She went to the dresser and picked up her hair brush. "I think my doll needs a haircut."

She sat the doll on her dresser and started brushing her hair.

"You better not cut her hair," Jill warned. "Mom will get mad. We just got our dolls last Christmas."

"Why would mom get mad?" Becky asked. "She cuts hair all the time."

"I cut one of my Barbie's hair really short," Michelle told them. "Sometimes I use that Barbie as a boy because I only have one Ken doll."

"I won't cut it too short," Becky assured Jill. "Just short enough so our dolls don't look the same."

"They don't look just alike. Mine has brown hair like me and yours has red hair like you." She held the dolls side-by-side.

"I'm going to cut it," Becky decided.

"When Mom sees your doll, don't forget I warned you," Jill shook her finger at Becky.

Becky went to the kitchen and found a pair of scissors in the junk drawer. In the bathroom she grabbed a hand towel and one of her mom's hair clippies.

Jill and Michelle watched her wrap the towel around the doll and use the clippie to hold it in place. "See, just like mom does hair," she told them.

She brushed the hair straight down.

Jill saw where she was holding the scissors against the doll's hair. "Becky, that looks pretty short."

Too late. *Snip!* A long strand of red hair fell on the dresser. Becky stood back to examine her work.

"That is kinda short, hmm?"

"You can't cut just one side," Michelle told Becky. Becky cut the other side. Now that side was shorter than the first side she had cut. She cut the first side again.

"That's better," Jill said. "You're not leaving the back, are you?"

Snip! Off came the back.

"Wow! That's really short," Michelle said.

"Mom holds the hair like this when she cuts," Becky said, holding it straight out from the doll's head. *Snip, snip, snip.*

"You better stop cutting. Your doll is going to be bald!" Jill warned.

"What on Earth!"

The girls turned to see Judy standing in the doorway.

"I thought you were working Mommy!" Becky said a little nervously.

"Becky Lou, why would you cut off your doll's pretty hair?"

"It's still pretty," Becky insisted.

"Yeah, pretty short!" Her mom stared at Becky's doll. "Clean up your mess. We will talk about this later." Judy left the room.

"Uh, oh," Michelle said.

"Yeah," agreed Jill.

"It's my doll!" Becky reminded them. "I like her short hair."

At supper Becky got a long lecture from her mom about how real people's hair grows back, but a doll's hair doesn't. Mom was not happy with Becky!

By morning, the rain had stopped and the sky had cleared. It was a hot and humid summer morning. That didn't help warm the water in the pool, though. It was even colder than usual.

"I don't know which is worse," Becky told Shari and Sivi. "Freezing in the water or sweating when you get out of the pool."

"Tomorrow can only be better," Shari hoped.

Today they would get to go off the diving board at the deep end of the pool. Becky was nervous. Kim, the life guard, was treading water in the pit while Becky stood on the board looking down at her.

"It's okay," Kim called up to Becky. "I'll be here if you need help. When you jump, you'll go under water. Your body will float back to the top, then you can swim to the side like we practiced."

Becky looked behind her at the other kids waiting in line. Jason and Shari gave her a thumbs-up.

"Come on, Becky," Scotty yelled from the side of the pool. "If I can do it, you can do it."

Sean had jumped off the board right before Becky's turn. He climbed out of the pool and stood beside Scotty. "It's fun."

Becky held her nose, took a deep breath and jumped. Before she fell in the water, she thought, *I hope I don't land on Kim.*

Becky's head popped out of the water. She felt Kim's hand on her back, turning her toward the side of the pool. She began kicking her legs and moving her arms. Her hand touched the concrete edge.

"I did it!" She grinned at Scotty and Sean. "Let's get back in line. I want to jump again."

On Friday Becky took her swimming test and passed with flying colors. She received her Level 2 Red Cross Certificate. Becky couldn't wait to show her mom and dad. Jill, J.R., Jason and Michelle passed their classes, too. Next year they would all advance to the next level.

Becky sat beside Betty on the way home. Betty's belly almost touched the steering wheel. "Are you going to have the baby soon?

You're getting really big." She put her hand between the steering wheel and Betty's stomach. "There's not much room left."

"I'll drive home if you want, Mom," J.R. volunteered, leaning forward to see around Becky.

"I can drive." Becky scooted up to the edge of the seat so she could see over the dash. She put her hand on the wheel. Betty let her steer the car. "It's easier to reach when I sit on Daddy's lap."

"Mom doesn't have any lap left," J.R. pointed out.

"I want to drive," Michelle said from the backseat.

"When we get home, you kids can drive around the block," Betty said.

They didn't let her forget, either. Luckily, Earl was home, so they drove his truck while Betty went inside.

J.R. took off on his motorcycle, but the others took turns sitting on Earl's lap and driving around the two blocks of Nettleton.

Earl parked in front of the Wilson house. Jason climbed off his lap. Earl got out with the kids and walked over to where Leon stood on the patio.

"What's going on, Wilson?"

Leon pointed toward the railroad tracks. "J.R. is trying to ride the rails on his motorcycle. That boy is going to break his arm riding that thing one of these days!"

Earl turned to watch J.R. "He's not doing too bad, is he?"

"He almost made it the whole block last time," Leon told his buddy. "I thought he was going to wipe out when his back tire fell of the rail, but he just turned around and tried again."

"Becky tells me Jason thinks he's Evel Knievel," Earl said. "Been popping wheelies."

"Yeah, J.R.'s been giving him pointers."

"He wanted to pop a wheelie when I rode with him the other day, but I said no," Becky told her dad.

"I think maybe you better not ride with Jason anymore, Beck," Earl told her. "He's getting a bit risky."

Chapter Ten

The Clubhouse

On Sunday, Becky wore to church the light blue dress her Great-aunt Edna Bell had made for her school pictures. It was her favorite dress. Today she would get assigned a new Sunday school teacher. She hoped it would be Frances Clarkson as she had requested. Frances is so nice and fun.

"Mom, can I ride my skateboard to church?" Becky walked into her mom's bedroom.

"In a dress? No, Becky, you will ride with us," her mom slipped on her shoes. "When we get home, I want you to clean the hamster cage and Jill to clean her fish bowl."

Mom rushed them out the door, running late as usual.

Becky's new teacher was Frances. Their first project was to make Noah's Arc figurines while learning about how God flooded the lands. This was so much better than her last teacher. All they had done was copy verses all year.

After church and lunch, Judy reminded them to clean the hamster cage and fish bowl.

Becky moved Muffin to the roll-around hamster ball while she emptied the water bottle and refilled it. She dumped the old bedding and spread new in the bottom of the cage. Speedy kept running on the wheel while she did her chore.

When she had it all cleaned, she opened the ball to put Muffin back in the cage.

"What's that?" Jill pointed to the little pink balls on the floor.

Becky leaned closer. "It's babies. Muffin had babies! Mom! Dad! Muffin had babies."

Earl and Judy came from the kitchen.

"What? How many?" Earl got down on his hands and knees.

"Should we put them in the cage?" Becky asked her dad.

"I see five hamsters," Mom said. "No, don't move them. Muffin will probably not want you to touch her babies. Jill, run grab some toilet paper for a nest. That should be soft enough for the babies."

"What should I do, Mom?" Becky asked.

"Well, if she's like any other new mom, she's going to be hungry. Let's boil a couple of eggs," Judy suggested.

Jill came back with the toilet paper. They folded it into a pile and put it in the corner of the main cage.

"We better keep Speedy away from the babies." Earl pulled off one end of a tunnel and put a cap on it. "Put some food and water at that end of the cage for Speedy," he told Becky.

"Hey, look," Jill said. "Muffin is moving her babies."

By the time Muffin had all the babies moved into the cage, the eggs were boiled. After they fed Muffin, Judy looked at Jill.

"Did you get your fish's bowl cleaned?"

"Well..."

"Get it done, Poon," Earl ordered. "I'll help you dump the water." Earl carried the bowl to the kitchen sink. Jill helped him hold the bowl sideways, letting the water run down the drain.

The phone rang. Judy picked up the receiver from the phone on the kitchen wall and walked back into the living room. The phone has a really long cord. "Hello?" they heard her answer from the other room.

But the ringing of the phone had startled Earl and Jill. They accidentally tilted the fish bowl too far, and Jill's black suckerfish went down the drain.

"Daddy!" Jill cried. "Get him back!"

"Oh, honey," Earl set the empty bowl on the counter. "I'm sorry. There's no way to get to him."

Judy walked back in the kitchen and hung up the phone. "What happened? Why is Jill crying?"

Becky came into the kitchen to get water for Speedy's side of the cage.

"We accidently dumped Jill's fish down the drain," Earl told his wife. "He's headed to Breckenridge now." Earl put his hand to his forehead and saluted. Earl had been in the Navy when he met Judy.

"I'm going to tell Grandma about my fish," Jill told her parents, leaving out the back door in the kitchen.

"It's okay," Becky heard her mom tell her dad. "She'll get over it. Accidents happen."

By supper, Jill's sad mood had lifted. Grandma had a way of always making the girls feel better.

Earl poured the last bottle of Dr. Pepper into two cups for himself and Judy.

"I want the last of it, Daddy." Jill reached for the glass bottle, tilting it up to empty the last few drops into her mouth.

"I wanted that!" Becky said. "It was my turn. You got it last time."

"You should have been faster."

"You aren't being fair."

"It's gone now," Jill held the bottle in front of Becky's face, tilting it back and forth.

Becky went to grab the bottle.

Jill reached for Becky's hair.

"Jill!" Judy yelled sharply.

Jill let go of the bottle and ran to the bathroom, slamming the door.

Judy had a WPFA meeting at The Clubhouse Wednesday afternoon. The members exchanged secret pal gifts, talked about events in the area, and had a potluck dinner. Sometimes they would sew or make craft projects.

Becky loved the old brick building. Leola, the woman who owned the building, allowed them the use The Clubhouse and was also a member. When you walked through the double glass doors, you entered a big room full of mismatched, donated furniture. On the left side, in the back of the room was a big table and chairs. Behind the table was a kitchen. In the back of the big room on the right was a curtain held up with a wire strung across the opening. On the other side of the curtain was Leola's son's fully restored two-seater surrey buggy.

Becky went with her mom to the meeting, but Jill stayed home with their dad. Becky's Great-Grandma Ollie, the secretary of the club, read the minutes from the previous meeting. Ruby, the current president, asked if there was any new business to discuss.

"I'd like to suggest a baby shower for Betty?" Beulah Faye spoke up.

Many of the ladies nodded.

Becky, Michelle and Cheryl were sitting at the table playing with sewing cards. Becky was threading her plastic needle with yarn when she heard them mention Betty's baby. That got her attention!

"Your due date is soon, right, Betty?" Patricia asked.

Betty nodded. "About two weeks."

"I propose setting a date for the baby shower on July 7th," Janice said, looking at her pocket calendar. "The baby, if it arrives as predicted, should be about a week old."

"I second the motion," Becky's Grandma raised her hand.

"All in favor?" Ruby asked.

All hands were raised, including Becky's.

Becky wasn't going to miss the baby shower for anything. She went to stand by her mom, tapping her on the shoulder. "Mom, can I go shopping with you to get the baby's present?"

"Not now, Becky," her mom whispered. "We'll talk about it later at home."

Becky went back to sit at the table. She picked up her elephant sewing card and poked her needle through the first hole, but she still listened to the ladies' meeting in case they mentioned the baby again.

Sylvia said, "The men are in the fields. I propose..."

Becky leaned closer to Michelle. "Let's go look at the buggy."

"We'll get in trouble," Michelle whispered back.

Becky shrugged her shoulders. "We're not going to tear it up. I want to sit in it."

They snuck behind the curtain. Becky climbed onto the seat of the dusty buggy. She stretched her hand up to the cover.

"I love the fringe on the roof." She ran her hands back and forth across the dangling strings.

Cheryl acted like she was holding the reins. "Giddy-up horsey. Let's go."

"Shhhh," Michelle reminded her. She sat between Becky and Cheryl.

"I need an umbrella," Becky said. "We could be ladies out for a Sunday buggy ride in the park."

The curtain swung back. There stood Sylvia. The three girls had guilty looks on their faces when they turned to face her.

"Now," Sylvia dragged out the word, "are you supposed to be back here?"

They shook their heads.

"Come on. It's time to eat." Sylvia ushered them back into the main area. "Clean your sewing boards off the table."

Chapter Eleven

The Sidewalk Surfers

After riding lessons on Monday, Becky and Jill took their skateboards to the Wilson's. For once, J.R., Jason and Michelle were all home.

Becky told the boys about the skateboard club. "We can call our club Sidewalk Surfers."

The boys were all in when she told them they could have races on the sidewalk at Clarkson's store.

They grabbed their skateboards to take to Clarkson's.

Manley was driving by and stopped his Impala in front of the house. "Where you kids headed?" he asked the group.

J.R. pointed to the store. "We're having a club meeting, Grandpa."

"Well, hop on," Manley said. "I'll give you a ride." J.R. and Jill hopped on the hood of the car, while Becky, Michelle and Jason sat on the trunk lid.

As they passed Blakely's trailer, they noticed several men in the yard. They were removing the skirting. A big tractor was parked beside the trailer.

Manley pulled into Clarkson's parking lot and they jumped to the ground. "Thanks, Grandpa," Jason called.

Manley opened his door and put the tip of his cane on the gravel. Manley had gotten polio when he went to California back in the early 1940's. Because of the polio, he needed a brace and cane to walk. By the time Manley made his way slowly to Clarkson's front door, the kids were standing in front of the store discussing Blakely's trailer.

"Are they moving it today?" Jason asked.

"How would I know?" J.R. said. "It looks like they're going to."

"Let's get started," Michelle said.

The Sidewalk Surfer's meeting began, though they kept an eye on the activity across the road.

"We should have uniforms," Becky suggested.

"Like what?" Jason asked. "I'm not wearing pink girlie clothes."

"How about white shirts? Is that neutral enough for you?" Becky asked him.

"Maybe like the Dallas cowboy cheerleaders," Michelle suggested. "J.R. has a poster of them in his room."

"I'll look at it when we're done practicing," Becky said. Since she had started the club, she felt like the leader when it came to decision making.

They began practicing.

JR. had the best skateboard. It was thinner and set a little higher off the ground. The rest of the skateboards were made of thicker plastic. J.R. usually won most of their races. Also, he was the oldest of the group.

"Watch this." Jason took off on his skateboard. He built up speed and put both feet on the board, then slammed his back foot down to make it stop. The board popped up like it was doing a wheelie. He kicked the board around with his other foot like a pivot and headed back to where they were standing.

"Try that," he told them.

It took some practice, but they could all stop and pivot when they decided to quit for the day. They walked back to the Wilson house to look at J.R.'s poster.

"Look, Jill," Becky pointed at the poster. "The blue is about the same color as that dress Mom made me for the school play. Didn't she cut it up for scraps?"

"I think so," Jill wrinkled her brow, thinking.

"Let's go see." Michelle was going with them. The boys were not interested so long as they could still dress like a boy.

When they stepped outside, Blakely's trailer was being pulled by the tractor past the house. They stopped to watch until it crossed the tracks and turned onto Highway 36. It was headed for Hamilton.

J.R. and Jason had come outside to watch the trailer being moved.

"They are probably going to hit the gravel road when they get closer to Hamilton," J.R. commented.

The excitement was over, so the girls left for Becky and Jill's place. They found the scrap material in a bag in Judy's closet. Becky dumped the bag on their mom's bed. "These will work perfect!"

Each scrap was about two feet long and shiny royal blue.

Jill counted them. "There's twenty. That should be enough, right?"

Becky nodded. "We'll tie one around our neck. We can wrap one around each wrist, too. Let's find a white shirt."

Becky and Jill each had a white shirt.

"Oh, crap!" Becky held up her white shirt. There was a big, faded orangish stain on the front. "I forgot about that. It's ketchup from the last time I wore it. Mom didn't think she was going to be able to get it out."

"Guess she was right," Michelle said.

"What about the yellow shirts we had to get for school?" Becky grabbed hers out of the closet. "J.R. and Jason should have these since every kid in grade school had to have one."

Jill was disappointed. She wanted to look as much like the Dallas Cowboy Cheerleaders as possible. "I suppose."

"It'll be okay," Michelle told Jill. "At least we'll all match."

Becky tossed Jill's shirt across the room. Jill put it on and tied the tails of the shirt together so her belly showed. "Just like the cheerleaders." She stood in front of the mirror, twisting from side to side. "Except for the color."

Becky tucked her shirt inside her shorts. "Let's go find your shirt," she told Michelle. They stuffed the rest of the material back in the bag and took it with them.

Michelle found her school shirt in her closet. When she was ready, they went to the boys' closet. The boys had taken off to who knows where, but Becky wanted to make sure everyone in the club had matching outfits.

"Here's J.R.'s," Jill pulled the hanger out of the closet.

"I found Jason's." Becky laid it on the bed.

Michelle pulled six strips out of the bag and handed them to Becky. Becky tied three on each hanger. She pushed the clothes in the closet to one side and hung the two shirts in the cleared space.

"If I don't see the boys before our club meets tomorrow," she told Michelle, "tell them where their shirts are, okay?"

They ran into the kitchen where Betty was washing dishes.

"Look, Mom," Michelle twirled around in a circle. "These are for our club."

"The Sidewalk Surfers," Becky clarified.

"Matching outfits," Betty smiled. "Is this a secret club?"

"No," Jill told her. "It's a skateboard club. We skateboard on the sidewalk at Clarkson's store."

"Oh, I see." Betty rinsed a plate and placed it with the other clean dishes on the towel spread on the counter.

Michelle walked around the counter and found the Dixie cup with her name written on the bottom.

Betty turned on the cold water. Becky and Jill picked out their cups, drank their water and put them back on the counter upside down.

"Bye, Mom," Michelle called.

"Bye, Betty." Becky and Jill followed her outside.

"Let's show your mom our outfits," Michelle said.

They took the shortcut to Judy's salon. Across the street, through Orie's yard and along Shaney's fence.

"Mom, look at our club uniforms," Jill said when they burst through the door of Judy's little salon. They twirled in a circle, showing off their outfits.

Judy was giving Scotty's mom, Jan, a haircut. "I like them. Is this for your skateboard club?"

The girls nodded.

"Did you hear the tractor?" Jill asked. "It pulled Blakely's trailer away. They have officially moved."

"Is that what we were hearing?" Judy asked. "We thought it was a farmer."

"Becky," Jan said. "I'm glad you stopped in while I was here. I was going to tell you before I left that your guitar is waiting for you at Clarkson's. They were just delivered earlier today. I picked Scotty's up on my way here."

Becky shrieked with excitement and clapped her hands. "I'm going to Clarkson's, Mom."

Becky had worked hard selling boxes of greeting cards around town to earn the guitar through the card prize program. She had been waiting so long to get the guitar, she'd almost forgotten about it.

She abandoned Jill and Michelle and ran all the way to the store.

Frances must have seen her coming. She had the guitar laying on the counter.

"Let me guess, you are here to pick up a guitar," Frances teased Becky.

Becky grinned. "Jan told me it was here."

"The delivery truck came right after you kids left earlier," Frances told her. "I figured you would be back soon."

"Thank you." Becky took the guitar home.

Becky sat outside on the front steps of the trailer and swung the guitar to her lap. Her hands automatically went into position, just like Roy Clark on "Hee Haw." Her fingers moved on the strings just like Roy's fingers on his guitar. But when Roy played the guitar, it sounded good. Becky's playing sounded horrible! She tried again. Bad. Really bad!

Jill and Michelle came around the corner of the trailer from the backyard. "Did you make that noise?" Jill asked.

"Yes," Becky said in disgust. "It's awful. I thought when you played the guitar, it always sounded good. Like your grandma's old self-playing piano," she nodded her head toward Michelle. "This makes me mad. I don't know how to play a guitar, after all. I sold all those greeting cards for nothing!"

Becky picked up the guitar and went behind the house to talk to her mom.

"I can't play it," Becky put the guitar in the dryer chair.

"Of course, you can't right off the bat, Becky," her mom told her. "You have to practice."

"I forgot to tell you earlier," Jan said. "Scotty lost his hamster."

This was a good distraction for Becky. "In the house?"

Jan nodded. "Last week. We haven't found it yet."

"Daddy brought home a boy hamster and now we have hamster babies."

Jan laughed and held out her hand. "Stop right there. I do not want one of the babies. We'd end up with two lost hamsters running loose."

Becky grinned. She looked down and saw her guitar. The smile faded. "I guess I'll go practice."

Chapter Twelve

"It's Not Funny!"

Thursday after work, Judy took Becky to her friend, Sivi's, house to spend the night. Sivi was waiting for her in the driveway. The girls ran to the backyard while Judy went inside to visit with Sivi's mom, Ada.

"How are your riding lessons going?" Sivi asked.

"Good," Becky said. She stopped at the fence surrounding the pasture. Sivi's horse, Brownie, came to greet her. Becky held out her hand to the horse. He nuzzled her hand, looking for his treat. "We've only had a few lessons, but I get better each week."

"I exercise Brownie every morning," Sivi said. "You and I can go for a ride tomorrow morning."

"I want to see Tigon," Becky told Sivi, giving Brownie a final pat on the nose. "Is she in the house?"

Sivi nodded, and they ran to the back door.

Tigon was playing on the living room floor with toys scattered around her. Judy and Ada were sitting on the sofa talking.

Becky reached down and picked up Tigon. "You have grown," she settled Tigon on her hip. "You're getting big."

Tigon squirmed to be let down. Becky was disappointed. She loved to carry Tigon around.

"Yeah," Sivi told her as they went upstairs to Sivi's bedroom. "She's too busy to let you hold her, now. She's always running around and climbing on everything."

Sivi picked up her baby doll. "Do you want to play dolls?"

"I guess," Becky said. "Even though my favorite red-haired doll won't play with me."

Sivi grinned and handed Becky the doll. "Tigon might play with you after her supper. She's not as gung-ho and full of energy then."

The girls played dolls for a bit, then took Sivi's new Connect Four game to the back deck.

Sivi kept winning until Becky got the hang of the game. They were in the middle of a serious competition when Tage, Sivi's other sister, came outside.

"I want to play," Tage said.

"Go play with Tigon," Sivi told her.

"I want to play with you," Tage insisted.

"Wait until we are done with this game, then we'll play Hide-n-Seek with you," Becky compromised.

At dinner, Becky found out what Sivi meant about Tigon always climbing. She used the handles on the drawers in the kitchen to try to climb onto the counters. Ada would put her back on the floor, then she would immediately start climbing them again. Sivi's mom finally put Tigon in her highchair and gave her a cracker.

After dinner, the girls went to Sivi's room. Becky climbed up to the top bunk. She did not expect to see a racoon. The racoon wasn't expecting to see Becky, either. It hissed at Becky. Becky jumped off the bed, hurting her leg.

Sivi laughed and laughed. "The look on your face was priceless. You should have seen it."

"Why didn't you tell me you had a racoon?" Becky rubbed her leg. It really hurt.

Sivi kept laughing. "That was so funny!"

Becky was starting to get a bit mad at Sivi. She wouldn't stop laughing! Becky stood up and tried to walk. She could walk, so her leg wasn't broken, but she did limp. It didn't hurt as bad when she moved around.

Sivi saw her limping and finally stopped laughing. "Did you hurt your leg?"

Becky nodded. "It's getting better."

At Becky's request, Sivi removed her pet racoon from the bedroom.

"Just in case he still thinks I'm the enemy," Becky told her friend.

Sivi started laughing again just thinking about it.

Becky glared at her.

"It was funny!" Sivi said in her defense.

After breakfast the next morning, they rode the horses. Sivi let Becky ride Brownie. They rode around the trees at the back of the property and all over the pasture. Becky wasn't ready for riding on a horse while it ran, but she could handle trotting.

They were riding in the back yard, closer to the house, when Sivi yelled, "Watch out!"

Becky had been daydreaming, staring off into space. She came back to reality and looked up. She jerked Brownie's reins to the left.

"You barely missed the clothesline," Sivi told her. "You would have fallen off Brownie."

"You probably would have laughed," Becky said, thinking of the racoon.

"Maybe," Sivi grinned

Chapter Thirteen

An Irish Red Head

Becky and Jill had their riding lessons on Saturday because Sue had something else she had to do on Monday. After riding lessons, Sue would have to leave for work. She worked as a bartender at Pringle's restaurant in Cameron. Their mom had to work, too, but assured Sue she would be back to get them before Sue needed to leave.

Today's riding lesson was on controlling Smokey using your legs.

Sue explained to them how to use their seat-bone and the calf of their legs to have Smokey move left or right.

As usual, Becky did her lesson first. Smokey did not go left like Becky wanted her to. "I think he's confused," she told Sue.

"Let's get a drink, then we'll try again."

Sue held the water hose while the girls drank.

"Are you ready to try again?"

Becky nodded.

She finally got the hang of guiding Smokey using body language. By the end of the lesson, she had Smokey turning easily using her legs.

She watched Jill practice on Smokey. Jill figured the motions out much quicker than Becky had. Of course, she had watched everything Becky had done during her lesson. She avoided the mistakes Becky had made and had Smokey moving all over the corral.

When the lessons were over, the girls helped Sue brush and feed Smokey. They put the supplies away. Judy still wasn't back to pick them up.

Sue looked at her watch. "I really need to leave now to get to work on time," she told the girls.

"Go ahead and leave," Becky told her. "Mom is always late."

"She'll be here soon," Jill assured Sue.

"Are you sure you'll be okay?" Sue was worried about leaving them alone.

"We stay home alone all the time. We'll be fine."

"Go to work," Jill insisted. "We're okay."

"Alright. I'm sorry, girls, but I need to leave."

Becky and Jill waited for their mom. And waited. And waited. Becky kept checking her Strawberry Shortcake watch. "Where is she?" Becky was getting mad. Mom was always late. But two hours!

"Maybe she is doing a color on a lady?" Jill tried to make excuses for their mom. "She could have a flat tire."

"I don't care," Becky yelled. "It's been two hours!"

Judy showed up not much later. "I'm sorry, girls. I was busy at work," Judy apologized. "Where's Sue?"

"She had to go to work right after our riding lessons," Jill answered.

"I'm sorry," Mom said again. "Get in the car and we'll go home."

"Two hours, Mom?" Becky snarled. She sat in the back seat with her arms crossed. She stewed all the way home.

"Now, Becky, I said I was sorry," her mom watched her in the rear-view mirror. "Don't let that red-headed Irish temper get out of control."

Becky continued giving her mom the silent treatment, turning her head to look out the window.

Becky and Jill did not go to church on Sunday. Instead, their mom woke them up bright and early to go camping with their grandparents.

They had packed the night before, with Mom's help, everything they would need for two nights away from home. Their bags were already in the camper because Grandpa wanted to be ready to go after breakfast.

They ate their cereal as fast as they could, kissed their mom good-bye, and ran across the road.

Chapter Fourteen

Fish and Frogs

Grandpa's camper was the type that slid onto the back of his pick-up truck. Becky and Jill sat between their grandparents in the cab. It took several hours to reach the campground in south Missouri, but they sang songs along with the radio and Grandpa told them stories. The time passed quickly.

When they reached the campsite, Becky was put in charge of collecting sticks for the campfire.

"Is this enough, Grandpa?" Becky dropped the armload of wood by the firepit.

"I reckon we'll need more than that," Red told her. "Grab another batch, will you?"

Finally, the campsite was set up and stocked with enough wood for two nights. Red gathered the fishing poles.

Becky swung her pole over her head. The line went flying across the water. Jill's line went flying across Becky's.

"Hey!" Becky yelled. "You're going to tangle them."

"I didn't mean to," Jill defended herself. "The wind blew it."

Becky started reeling hers in. "Now look what you've done!" Becky's hook was caught on Jill's line. Jill walked closer to Becky.

"Don't move! You're going to make it worse." Becky laid her fishing pole on the ground. She followed the line with her hand until she reached the hook. "It's stuck. Grandpa!"

Red came over to see what the problem was. "Here," he took the hook from Becky, "let me try."

"It's Jill's fault. She threw her line right across mine," she told her grandpa. "She didn't even look. Now we'll never get to catch any fish."

"Why is it my fault?" Jill retorted. "I was just casting my line. I couldn't help it if the wind was blowing."

"Yes, you could," Becky said. "You should have gone over there." She pointed to the edge of the clearing.

"I'm not standing in the weeds to fish," Jill shot back. "You stand over there!"

"I was here first."

"I was here first."

"I put mine is the water first!"

"Girls!" Red stopped the arguing. "Here," he handed Becky her fishing pole. "It's untangled. Go ahead and reel in your line."

Red moved Becky down the shore some ways and stood between them.

"I've got one. Grandpa, help!" Jill yelled, pulling back on her fishing pole.

"I'm coming." Red laid his fishing pole in the crook of the stick he had poked in the ground and went to help Jill. "Steady, keep cranking. Here he comes."

Jill's fish was flopping in the air, dangling by the hook in its mouth.

Becky went to see the fish. "It's a small one. You have to throw the small fish back so they can keep growing."

"That's right," Red agreed, glad she had remembered his instructions from previous fishing trips. "And what else?"

"Try not to touch the fish any more than you have to," Jill recited.

Red removed the hook from the fish's mouth and tossed it back into the lake.

Becky caught one fish barely big enough to keep and Jill caught two more little fish that had to be thrown back into the lake. They put away their fishing poles and played in the shallows looking for tadpoles while their grandpa and grandma continued fishing.

"Here's one," Jill pointed in the water.

"If we catch it, maybe Grandpa will let us keep it," Becky told her sister. "We can put it in a bowl and watch it turn into a frog."

They tried to catch the tadpole, but he kept darting away.

"I've got him," Becky said. She had him trapped in her cupped hands under water. "Find something to put him in, Jill."

Jill ran to the camper. "What are you looking for?" Grandma asked.

Jill opened the cabinet under the little sink. "We need a bowl for our tadpole."

"Let's leave the bowl for a minute." Grandma guided Jill back out of the camper and down to the water.

Becky was still squatting in the shallow water. "Did you get the bowl?"

"There are a lot of tadpoles in the water, aren't there?" Grandma asked.

Becky twisted her head around to see Grandma standing behind her. She nodded.

"Do you want to see ours?" Becky started to lift her hands holding the little tadpole.

"No. What I'm thinking is that the other tadpoles are probably brothers and sisters of the one you caught."

Becky craned her neck around to look back up at her grandma. "You want us to let it go, don't you?"

"Don't you think that's the nice thing to do?" Grandma waited for an answer.

"I guess," Jill said, disappointed.

"But we want to watch it turn into a frog," Becky tried to sway her grandma.

"And then what?"

"And then we let it go," Becky told her.

"By the time it turns into a frog, we will be back home. You will have to hold the bowl all the way home on your lap. When you let it go, the frog will be at our home, but his brothers and sisters will be here, at his home." Grandma was giving them something to think about. "If it was you, would you like to be that far away from home?"

"No," Becky shook her head. She let the tadpole loose and stood up, drying her hands on her shirt.

Jill pointed at Becky's butt and grinned. "You're butt's wet. It looks like you peed your pants."

"I didn't pee my pants!" Becky exclaimed.

"Yes, you did," Jill laughed and started singing. "Becky peed her pants, Becky peed her pants."

"Grandma, make her stop."

"Becky peed her pants," Jill continued. Becky had had enough. She went for Jill, arms stretched out in front of her. Jill took off running, still singing. They ran around the firepit, around the camper and back to the water. Jill kept running but Becky stopped.

"Now who's wet?" Becky called from the shore.

The girls wanted to sleep outside in sleeping bags around the fire, but the mosquitoes were so bad they slept on the lowered table in the camper instead. Grandpa Red and Grandma Betty slept above the cab.

Becky woke up when the camper door shut. She leaned up on one elbow and looked around. She was alone but she could hear the others talking outside. Taking her blanket with her, she left the camper. It was chilly this morning. She wrapped the blanket around her and sat in an empty folding chair.

"Morning, Sleepyhead," Red called out cheerfully. "Are you hungry? Grandma's cooking up some pancakes this morning." Red rolled his pancake around a sausage link and took a bite.

Jill accepted the green plate from her grandma. Betty had four sets of camping plates, bowls and cups. Each set was a different color. Becky always used the red set and Jill always had the green set.

"Want some coffee?" Red held out his blue mug for Becky.

"Yuck, Grandpa," Becky wrinkled her nose.

"Jill?" he tried again.

"He's teasing you kids," Betty handed them their matching mugs. "I made you hot chocolate."

"I love chocolate," Becky held the cup under her chin and enjoyed the hot steam floating up towards her face.

"What are we doing today, Grandpa?" Jill asked.

"Today your Grandma is taking you in to town to go shopping while I fish."

So, the girls spent the morning looking in store windows in the small town just down the road from the campground. Their grandma picked up a few groceries at the little country store. The girls blew bubbles with the gum she bought them.

"Look at this, Grandma," Becky pointed to the frog statue in a store window display.

"Isn't it cute?" Jill said. "It's the same size as a real frog."

"Let's go inside," Grandma ushered them into the store. "It will be a good memento for you to remember this camping trip."

They showed their grandpa the polished frog when they returned to the campsite.

"This one isn't slimy or stinky," Jill told him.

"No water needed," Becky added. "I won't mind holding him on my lap all the way home, either."

After lunch, the girls caught a couple of frogs.

"Let's have a frog jumping contest," Jill suggested.

Becky held both frogs in her rolled up shirt bottom while Jill found branches to drag into the clearing. They arranged the branches parallel about two feet apart. Becky handed Jill her frog.

They sat both frogs at one end and held them in place with their hands.

"On your mark, get set, go!" Becky called out.

They moved their hands away from the frogs.

"Go, frog. Jump!" Jill smacked the ground behind the frog. Both frogs jumped, trying to get over the logs.

"That way," Becky encouraged, pointing to the other end of the branches. "Go that way. Jump."

Before long, they realized this contest was never going to end. Jill's frog jumped around in a complete circle and finally got stuck against the underside of a branch. Becky's frog jumped a few inches and wouldn't budge for anything.

"I give up," Becky said. She stood up and brushed the dirt off her shorts.

"I'd rather play in the water." Jill leaned over and rinsed her hands at the edge of the lake.

"I'm glad our campsite is shady," Becky lifted her pigtails off her neck. "It's getting hot."

They splashed in the shallow water, chasing each other and chasing fish. Red had moved to the other side of the weedy area long ago because, as he said, "You're scaring away all the fish!"

Way after the moon came out and it got dark, they sat around the campfire.

"I'm staying up all night," Becky told her grandparents. "I can sleep on the way home in the morning."

"Think you can stay awake that long?" her grandpa asked.

"I can," Jill told him.

"Me, too," Becky said.

Betty pulled out a book and a flashlight. The book was 'Mr. Punnymoon's Train.'

"I brought a book to read," Grandma said. She ruffled Jill's hair. "You do know your dad calls you 'Poon' because this is your favorite book, right?"

Becky liked Mr. Punnymoon, too.

An hour later, they were carried into the camper and put to bed.

Chapter Fifteen

Little People and Races

The camper pulled into the driveway the next day before lunch time.

"I'm glad to be home," Betty said. She opened the door of the cramped truck.

Becky and Jill climbed out and headed across the street.

"Come back later and get your stuff," Grandma called. "I'll have it unloaded."

"We will," they promised.

The first thing they saw when they came around the corner of the trailer was their dad's baby blue pick-up.

"Daddy's home," Jill stated.

Earl must have seen them coming. He stepped out of the house on the front porch. "I'm home until Monday." They ran up the steps and gave him a big hug.

"Did you have a good trip?"

"Oh, yes," Jill told him. She wrapped her arms around his neck and he stood up, holding her. "We like going camping with Grandpa and Grandma."

Becky nodded. "I'm going to go see Mom, then I'm going to Michelle's."

"Go ahead," Daddy said, putting Jill down. "I'm going over to talk to your grandparents."

"I'm going with Becky," Jill told him.

Their mom was in her beauty salon. They didn't stay to visit with her for long.

Becky was both disappointed and relieved to find Betty still pregnant when they walked into the Wilson house. Disappointed not to meet the baby, but relieved Betty hadn't given birth while they were camping.

Michelle must have heard them in the living room. She came out of her bedroom. "How was camping?"

"It was fun," Jill told her. "But it was a long drive. What did you do while we were gone?"

"My dad came home and we went to Roach Lake. The Pratt's went with us and we rode in dad's boat," Michelle told them. "I'm playing Little People. Come on, they are all set up."

Becky and Jill followed Michelle to her room. Michelle had set up most of her Fisher Price Little People toys. She'd even brought all J.R.'s and Jason's into her room.

Jill sat in front of the castle. "The Queen is having a dinner party. She needs invitations delivered."

"I'll be the postman." Becky drove the mail truck to the castle and picked up all the little plastic cards. She drove them around the town and put them in the mail slots.

Michelle turned the light signal at the crossing to red. Becky ran through the red light. Michelle grabbed the police car and chased her.

Becky stopped at the school. "Let's have the kids go to school."

Jill sorted through the box until she found six Little People kids. "Maybe they should take a field trip to the circus. Michelle, where's the train with the animals?"

"I forgot to get it out." Michelle went in her closet. She tossed out the elephant and the giraffe. "I can't find the monkey." She walked out with the train and the merry-go-round.

"Here's the monkey," Jill held it up. "It was stuck in the dungeon of the castle."

Becky pushed the button on the train. *Choo, choo*, the whistle blew.

Jason came into the bedroom. "Why do you have my garage?"

"We're playing with it," Becky told him. "We have J.R.'s airport, too."

"I want my garage back."

"Just play with us," Jill said. "It's all set up."

For once, Jason didn't argue. He drove the yellow car from its parking spot on top of the garage to the elevator. Down it went. He drove it to the gas pump.

Betty stepped into the bedroom an hour later. "Your mom called. Time to go home," she told Becky and Jill.

During supper, they told their parents all about their camping trip even though their dad had probably heard the details from his parents already.

"Did Grandma give you our frog figurine?" Jill asked her dad.

Earl nodded, chewing a bite of his hamburger. He swallowed and took a drink of milk. "I put it on your dresser."

"Do you want to come to our Sidewalk Surfers meeting, Daddy?" Becky asked. "We meet tomorrow morning. You can see all we've learned to do on our skateboards."

"I can't, Beck," Earl shook his head. "But if your meeting is at Clarkson's store, I'll be nearby."

"Why? What are you doing?" asked Jill.

"Me and a couple of guys are going to tear down that old house north of the store."

"The empty one?" Becky asked.

"That's the one," her dad nodded. "When I was a kid, a boy named Wayne lived in that house. Your friend Linda? Her parents lived there when they got married until right before she was born."

The next morning after breakfast, Becky and Jill went to the store to meet the Wilson kids. Jason and Michelle were sitting on the step of the old bank. They had on their club outfits.

"Where's J.R.?" Becky asked.

"He had to help Dad," Jason said. "He'll be here soon."

"I learned something new," Michelle stood up and put her skateboard on the sidewalk. "Watch this."

She stood on her skateboard, without it rolling, and flipped the back of the board around to the front, then flipped it again and again until she had "walked" about six feet away.

"I wanna try." Jill stepped on her skateboard.

"Have you learned to play your guitar yet?" Jason asked as they all tried walking their skateboards.

Becky wrinkled her nose. "It's not going too good."

J.R. slid up on his skateboard and saw what they were practicing. Of course, he immediately got the hang of it and did it better than all of them. At least he was wearing his club clothes.

"Let's race," he said, bored with continuing to do a move he'd already mastered. "We'll start back there at the beginning of the sidewalk. When you get to the steps of the store you must leave both feet on your board. Whoever rolls the farthest wins."

This race sounded fair. Becky lined up with the others. They went one at a time.

"When you stop rolling," J.R. told them, "stay on your board so we know who wins."

Becky rolled to the second door after the store. Michelle was right behind her. Jill stopped beside Michelle. Jason stopped rolling about an inch farther. J.R. rolled past all of them.

"One of these days, I'm going to beat you," Becky told him.

"Yeah," he laughed. "The day I'm not here."

"I'll race you again right now," Becky challenged him.

"You're on!"

They were finishing the second race, which J.R. won, when Earl pulled up in his pick-up.

"I need to run to Chillicothe. Jump in, girls."

They put their skateboards in the back and waved good-bye.

"Why are we going to Chillicothe?" Jill asked.

"I need a few things for the demolition," he answered. "I figured if you girls wanted to go, we'd stop by Dairy Queen when I'm done."

"Yum," Becky licked her lips. "I want a chocolate ice cream cone."

Chapter Sixteen

Tenny and Theron Jon

Becky did get her chocolate ice cream cone. Jill chose strawberry. On their way home, they met Leon and Betty heading towards Chillicothe.

Earl grabbed the CB radio mic. "Breaker 1-9, breaker 1-9. You got your ears on Pinocchio? Come back." The CB crackled.

"This here's Pinocchio. That you, Daffy Duck? Come back." They heard Leon's voice over the air waves.

"Ten-four. Where you headed there? Come back."

"I think we're working on a stork run. Come back."

"Well, hot damn! Congratulations, good buddy. We'll talk to you on the flip side."

"That's a big then-four. Pinocchio over and out."

"What did that mean, Daddy?" Becky asked when Earl hung the mic back in its slot.

"That means Betty is having the baby," Earl grinned.

"Turn around!" Becky bounced in her seat. "We have to go to the hospital."

"It's tempting," Earl said. "But sometimes babies can take a long time even after you get to the hospital before they are born. Plus, they usually only let adults in to see the baby or the baby's brothers or sisters."

"Are you saying we can't see the baby at all until they bring him home?" Becky was outraged.

Earl nodded.

"But that's my baby. I've been waiting forever for Betty to have him."

"I'm sorry, Becky. That's the rules."

Earl dropped them off at the trailer before going back to work on the house they were demolishing.

Becky walked in behind Jill and slammed the door shut.

Judy was sitting on the couch sewing a shirt. "What's wrong, Becky Lou?"

"Betty's going to the hospital to have the baby and we can't see the baby until she comes home!"

"That's the hospital rules," Jill told their mom.

"It's not fair!" Becky protested.

"It is how it is," their mom said. "You've waited this long; another week won't kill you."

"A whole week? *Arghh!*" Becky threw her hands in the air and stomped to her bedroom.

Becky went to Michelle's house bright and early the next morning.

"It's a boy," Michelle said as soon as Becky walked into her bedroom.

"We heard. Daddy told us when Leon called last night." Becky sat on Michelle's bed. "Have you got to see him yet?"

"No," Michelle shook her head. "Dad is taking us to the hospital when he gets back from coffee at the Colonial Café. My Great-aunt

Goldie is staying with us until Mom comes home." Michelle scrunched her nose.

"Oh, she's your least favorite aunt, right?"

"Yeah," Michelle nodded. "It always seems that she only likes J.R. I have to share my room with her while she's here."

"Oh, sorry," Becky sympathized.

"It'll be okay." Michelle pecked at her little piano.

"Hey, here's an idea," Becky said. "What if the Sidewalk Surfers form a band. We can give your mom and the baby a concert when they come home. By the way, what did your parents name him?"

"Theron Jon."

"Theron Jon," Becky repeated. "We'll give Betty and Theron Jon a concert when they come home. We can use your dad's semi-trailer for our stage."

"I like it. Let's do it."

"Let's round up the others. Jill should be awake by now. I'll get my guitar."

"J.R. will probably sleep late and Jason went to town with Dad," Michelle said. "Remember, we're leaving when Dad gets home. I want to see my new baby brother."

"Me, too. It's not fair that I can't go," Becky frowned.

"We could tell them you're my sister," Michelle suggested.

"What about my red hair? All of you kids are blonde," Becky pointed out.

"My mom is a red head," Michelle reminded Becky.

"Duh. How could I have forgotten that!"

But when Leon and Jason got back from town, Earl was with them. "No, Becky," he said firmly. "You will wait until Betty comes home." And that was that.

The next day, Becky and Jill were playing Barbie's in the back yard when they heard a crash.

"What was that?" Jill asked.

"I think they finally got that old house to fall down," Becky guessed.

Becky had guessed right. Half an hour later their dad walked in the door while they were eating lunch. He was carrying a little ball of fur.

"What do you have there?" Becky stood up and went to look.

"It's a baby raccoon."

"He's so little and cute," Jill rubbed his head with her finger.

"Where did you find him?" Becky asked.

"He was in that house we tore down. The mom must have abandoned her babies. I already named him Tenny."

"We get to keep him?" They looked at their dad, hopefully.

"As long as it's okay with Mom."

"I hope Tenny likes me better than Sivi's racoon does," Becky worried.

Judy said 'yes' when they asked. Earl, on the other hand, got a lecture.

"No more animals after this," she shook her finger at him. "A two-bedroom trailer can only hold so many living creatures."

"Whatever you say, honey." He wrapped his arms around Judy and kissed her cheek.

"I mean it," she stated.

The girls filled a baby doll's bottle with milk and fed Tenny.

"That should keep Becky happy until Betty brings the baby home," Earl said, watching the girls fawn over the little racoon.

Chapter Seventeen

Accidents Galore

Becky was busy all week. Between the skateboarding, the band practices, the riding lessons and Tenny, the week went by quickly.

It also seemed to be the week for accidents. The first accident happened to J.R.

"Watch this," he told the others. He shoved his skateboard away from him with his foot, then ran to catch up to the board and tried to jump on it. Unfortunately, when his foot landed on the board, it shot out away from him. J.R.'s foot flew up in the air and his body crashed to the sidewalk. Thankfully he landed on his side instead of his head before skidding down the sidewalk.

Jason came over to examine J.R.'s bleeding arm. "It looks like you have road rash. You had better show Aunt Goldie."

They followed J.R. to his house. Jason carried J.R.'s skateboard for him.

Aunt Goldie clucked her tongue. She insisted on bandaging his arm, from wrist to elbow.

"Really, Aunt Goldie, I'm fine," J.R. tried to tell her. "Mom would just put Bactine on it."

"You need to stay inside for the rest of the day," Aunt Goldie told him.

"Why?" J.R. was incredulous. "I've been hurt way worse than this and didn't even need a Band-Aid."

Becky nodded. "That's true."

Aunt Goldie wouldn't budge. "You kids go on outside and let J.R. rest."

J.R. rolled his eyes behind Aunt Goldie's back and grabbed the television remote. "Have fun without me."

The next accident happened on Sunday at The Country Place. Earl and Judy decided to take all five kids- Becky, Jill, J.R., Jason and Michelle- to the skating rink over by Braymer. They usually went to The Country Place every Sunday in the winter, but in the summer, they didn't go as often. When Becky and Jill told them how strict Aunt Goldie was being with the Wilson kids, their parents figured they needed a break from their great aunt.

Great-aunt Goldie was reluctant to let the kids go skating, but Leon was home and offered to take her to see Betty at the hospital while the kids were gone. They all piled into Judy's Oldsmobile 442. Earl was in the driver's seat.

"I bet if your mom drove we would get there faster," Jason, sitting beside Becky, leaned over to whisper in her ear.

Everyone knew Judy had a lead foot. The other day when Becky was at Clarkson's store, she had heard the men sitting around the wood stove talking about her mom.

"When I see Judy coming, I just move my truck right over to the shoulder," Rufus had said.

"Betty and Jan are just as bad," Ralph had told him.

"Ain't that the truth," Orie had agreed. "Them three drive like three bats outta Hell. And the music! Betty must keep her radio cranked full volume."

So, Becky knew exactly what Jason was saying, but Earl got them there soon enough.

As usual, The Country Place was packed with people. Across the front of the building was the skate rental desk, the concession counter and tables for eating. At one end were the bathrooms. At the other end was the beginner's rink, which they called the baby rink. Down both sides of the long building were lots of tables. On the west side were pool tables and pinball machines. The disc jockey had a booth by the entrance for the rink on the same side. The middle of the building was the big skating area. At the far end of the rink were two stages for bands; one in each corner.

On Saturday nights, The Country Place would have dances and bring in bands; some famous singers, others local talent.

They went to the counter to get their skates then sat down and laced them. Judy helped tighten their laces. They had to sit on the east side by the baby rink because there were so many people. The west side usually filled up first because of the game tables.

Becky started skating in the baby rink. Jill and Michelle joined her. The baby rink has a smoother floor and is much smaller. There is a gate to go directly into the big rink from the baby rink.

"Hold my hands, Jill," Becky said. "Let's see how fast we can do circles."

Becky and Jill held hands in the middle of the baby rink. They shoved off and turned their skates so their toes pointed out. Around and around they went. Faster and faster. Their hands came apart, and they both fell.

"I think I'm warmed up," Becky said. "I'm going to the big one."

Becky was surprised to see her mom skating. Sometimes she would skate, other times she wouldn't. Becky skated closer to her mom.

"I'll race you," she offered.

"You go ahead," Mom said. "I'm still warming up."

Becky took off and caught up with Jason. They chased each other for a few laps.

The D.J. played the song *That's the Way*. Lots of skaters entered the rink. This song was popular, and the D.J. played it often. It had a good beat and the faster skaters liked to speed skate to the song. They would weave in and out of the slower skaters.

"We could sing this song at our concert for your mom and Theron Jon," Becky told Jason. "The words are easy enough."

"That's for sure," Jason agreed. "They get boring after a while."

"It does repeat a lot," Becky said. "We can just sing one chorus. I'll tell the others." She skated off to find Jill and Michelle.

They were still in the baby rink practicing skating backwards. Becky skated in front of Michelle and held out her hands. It was easier to skate backwards when you were first learning if someone held onto you. Then you could look over your shoulder to see where you were going and the other person would balance you. It was easier with them pushing you, too.

"We are going to sing this song at our concert," Becky told her. "Make sure you listen and memorize all of the chorus."

Right about then, the song ended.

"It's okay," Michelle said. "I know the song. Who doesn't? It's the same words over and over."

Jill was skating beside them. "We can request it again later."

"Okay," Becky said. "But don't request it until I tell J.R. so he can listen next time it plays."

The D.J. dimmed the lights and put on a slow song. "This is for all you lovebirds out there. Grab your special someone and get on the floor."

Becky knew the baby rink was about to get crowded. Every time the younger skaters couldn't use the big rink, the small baby rink filled up. She rolled to the red-carpeted bannister that ran along the edge of the big rink and leaned on it to watch the couples skate. Her mom and dad skated around and around.

"I'll skate with you, Becky."

She turned around to see a boy she had seen here the last few times she had been to The Country Place. She didn't know his name, but she knew he lived in Breckenridge. "Okay."

It turned out, his name was David and he knew her Grandpa.

"My dad takes his truck to Red to get the oil changed and I usually go with him," David told her. "I've seen you outside in your yard across the road when I go with Dad."

Becky couldn't ever remember seeing David anywhere but at The Country Place.

The song ended.

"All skate," the D.J. announced.

Becky let go of David's hand and skated back to where Jill and Michelle were standing at the bannister.

"Ohhh," Jill gushed. "Becky's got a boyfriend."

Michelle joined Jill in teasing Becky. "Becky's got a boyfriend."

"Shut up!" Becky told them. "I do not!" She skated away.

Becky had made a few laps around the rink when she saw her dad motioning her back to the table. The pizzas her dad had ordered were ready.

J.R. skated to the table and sat down. Now was a good time to tell him about the song.

Judy heard Becky talking about the concert. "You kids are practicing for a concert?"

They all nodded.

Jason swallowed his pizza. "We are going to sing for Mom and my new brother."

Earl laughed. "What a song to choose!"

Becky immediately got defensive. "It's easy. It's one of the favorite songs for skating."

"It's fine," Judy told them, giving Earl a stern look. "Betty will love it."

"Ladies and gents," they heard the D.J. announce, "let's all swing around for a backwards skate only."

"I want to skate backwards. I'm getting better." Jill put down her cup and stood up. "Come on, Michelle, push me."

They skated onto the floor.

"I need someone to push me," Becky said. She looked around the table. J.R. and Jason were still eating.

Her mom stood up. "Come on, Becky. But only you. I'm not taking turns. No backwards skating for me!"

Usually halfway through a song, they would switch places so the other person could skate backwards. Normally, Becky and Jill would be a pair, and Michelle would skate with Betty. Betty was a good skater and had her own skates.

The accident happened when Jill twisted around to look behind her at the same time Michelle sneezed, letting go of Jill's hand. Jill fell, banging her chin on the concrete floor and getting a bloody lip.

Unlike Great-aunt Goldie, Judy did not overreact. Thank God. She asked for ice at the concession counter. Jill sat around holding the towel filled with ice against her lip until the bleeding had stopped.

The next two accidents happened a couple of days later, but on the same day.

Becky, Jason and Michelle were riding their bikes around the block when they saw a car coming. They turned to ride on the sidewalk from the Baptist Church to the hotel. Jason wanted to jump the angled end of the sidewalk at the hotel next to the parking lot of Clarkson's store.

On the way, he kept popped wheelies. He popped a wheelie again, except this time his front tire missed the sidewalk, fell off the edge into the grass and he crashed. It wouldn't have been so bad, but somehow, he found maybe the only rock in the grass to land on. The rock scraped him right beside his eye and started to bleed.

Michelle happened to have one of her hankies her Great-aunt Mary had made in her pocket. She handed it to Becky.

Becky tried to make the bleeding stop, but it wouldn't. She finally just held it against Jason's face with her hand. "Maybe we should show your Aunt Goldie."

"No way," Jason replaced Becky's hand holding the handkerchief with his own. "It will stop bleeding soon. She'll make me stay in the house and Sidewalk Surfers have to practice later. Mom and the baby will be coming home soon, and we're almost ready for the concert."

"Let's go to Aunt Ada's and wash your face," Michelle suggested. They had just passed Aunt Ada's house when Jason wrecked.

Aunt Ada isn't really their aunt, but all the kids in town have always called her Aunt Ada.

Aunt Ada let them into the house. While she cleaned Jason's face in the kitchen, the girls wandered around her living room. Michelle picked up her little wind-up piano. She turned the knob, and the music started to play.

"I love this piano," Michelle said. "Aunt Ada always lets me play with this."

"I like her little animals." Becky was rubbing her fingers on the miniature dogs and cats. "They are so smooth."

Aunt Ada and Jason came in from the kitchen. Jason had a scratch about an inch long by his eye, but it was no longer bleeding.

"All better," Aunt Ada said.

"Maybe Aunt Goldie won't even notice," Jason said, hopefully.

Aunt Ada picked up her candy bowl and held it out to them. "Anyone want a butterscotch or peppermint?"

The second accident of the day was at Clarkson's store during Skateboard Surfers rehearsal. J.R. was following Jill, both on their skateboards, when Jill stopped suddenly and J.R. ran into her. His skateboard rammed into to her ankle.

Jill fell to the sidewalk and grabbed her ankle. She had tears in her eyes. "Ouch. Crap. Ouch. It hurts."

Becky's first thought was, *What will Daddy say? Will he take away our skateboards?*

But J.R. sat on the sidewalk by Jill and rubbed her ankle until it didn't hurt as much. When Jill stood up, she limped, but the pain was going away.

"Just sit on the step and watch us until the pain is totally gone, okay?" Jason told her.

"And watch for Daddy," Becky added.

But Jill's ankle quit hurting before practice was over, and soon she was back on her skateboard.

Somehow, when the day rolled around for Betty and Theron Jon to come home from the hospital, they were all still intact, other than some scratches and bruises. The concert could happen.

Chapter Eighteen

The Concert

When Michelle called to tell them her mom and the baby were home, Becky's mom wouldn't let her go to see the baby right away.

"Let Betty get the baby settled," she told the girls. "The hospital probably sent a lot of baby stuff home with them. We'll wait at least an hour."

Becky really tried to be patient. She watched television. She watched the hamsters. She played with Tenny. Finally, her mom said they could go to Betty's.

"I'll meet you there." Becky took off running out the back door with Jill at her heels. They took the shortcut.

Becky will probably never figure out how her mom beat her to Betty's house, but she did and they all walked in the house together. The Reverend was pulling out of the driveway, and the Pratt's were walking out the door.

Becky said to Jill, "I knew we could have come sooner."

Judy stopped to talk to Janice, but the girls rushed inside.

Betty was sitting in one of the matching orange recliners. Michelle was sitting on the couch holding the baby. Becky sat on one side of her and Jill on the other.

"He's so tiny," Becky cooed.

"That's what I thought," Michelle agreed. "Mom said he's a big baby. Over nine pounds."

"He looks small to me," Jill said.

"Look, his hair is kinda reddish like mine," Becky rubbed his head gently.

"You want to hold him?" Michelle offered. "He gets heavy after a while."

Becky nodded.

Judy had come in the house and sat down across the room. Now she stood up to help pass the baby, but she was too late. Michelle handed the baby to Becky.

"Be careful, Becky. Newborn babies are fragile," she warned.

Becky was totally in love with this baby. He was better than baby racoons, baby hamsters, baby bunnies and baby birds all put together.

She finally had to pass him to Jill, even though she wanted to keep holding him.

Michelle stood and went to her mom. She started to sit on her mom's lap.

"Now," Aunt Goldie stopped her. "Your mom is tender. You can't be jumping all over her."

Michelle sat on the arm of her mom's chair. "Sidewalk Surfers has been practicing. We're going to give you and Theron a concert tonight."

"You are?" Betty put her arm around Michelle and pulled her against her side, despite Aunt Goldie.

Becky said, "We've worked really hard. We're going to use Leon's trailer for the stage."

"When is the concert?" Betty asked.

"Right after supper tonight," Becky told her.

"I don't think tonight is a suitable time," Aunt Goldie said. "Betty needs to rest. Maybe tomorrow."

"I'll be there," Betty said.

"And Theron," Jill reminded Betty.

"We will both be there," Betty promised. "Come in and let me know when you're ready."

"We will."

Judy left to meet a client, but Becky and Jill stayed for most of the afternoon. Neighbors kept dropping by all day to see the baby and check on Betty. Some of them brought gifts for Theron Jon. Judy hadn't brought the gift they had helped her pick out. She was going to give it to Betty at the baby shower on Sunday.

When J.R. and Jason came in with their Grandma Helen, the Sidewalk Surfers started getting ready for the concert.

Leon usually parked his semi-truck and trailer in front of the house. Today he had moved it across from his parents' house because of all the company coming and going.

"I'll move it," J.R. said. "We need it parked at our house so we can bring out our instruments. We'll need an extension cord for the microphones, too."

"We have to scrounge up chairs for our parents to sit on," Jill said.

"You better not move Dad's truck, J.R.," Jason warned him. "Dad will beat your butt with his belt."

"Don't get in trouble today," Becky begged. "You'll ruin our concert."

"Fine," J.R. said. "I won't move the truck as long as he shows up soon."

"I'll go find Dad," Michelle offered hurriedly. Becky volunteered to go with her. Jason and Jill stayed to make sure J.R. didn't get impatient and move Leon's Kenworth.

Leon was at Joe's Garage standing around the bed of Freddie's pick-up truck talking to a few men and Becky's Uncle Sammy. When Becky and Michelle explained the situation, he agreed to move the truck.

"I'll be there soon," he promised.

"Don't wait too long," Becky warned him. "We had to talk J.R. out of moving it himself."

"He better not!" Leon turned to look across Joe's back yard to the next block where he had parked his semi. "I better go. I'll talk to you later," he told Becky's Uncle Sammy, Joe and the brothers, Cookie and Freddie.

"Congratulations again," Cookie hollered as he left.

Leon moved the truck to exactly where they wanted it. The kids began setting up their instruments.

"Are you going to be in the Fourth of July parade Saturday?" Becky asked Michelle.

"Yep," Michelle nodded. She arranged her electric piano and stool on one side of their stage. "Dad stopped at Walmart so we could pick out our streamers. I'm decorating mine in red and pink."

"So are we," Jill said. "I have blue and white streamers for my bike."

That night, after supper, Becky and Jill changed into their club outfits. Their mom and dad went with them to the Wilson's. They had a good-sized audience. Earl, Judy, and Earl's parents, Red and Betty were sitting by Leon, Betty and Leon's parent's, Manley and Helen. Uncle Sammy and Aunt Goldie were waiting for the concert to begin, also. Betty was holding Theron Jon in her arms.

Becky assumed the role of announcer. "On the drums we have Jason." Jason beat on every drum, snagged the symbol and thumped the bass drum with his foot.

"On the keyboard we have Michelle." Michelle played a chord her Great-aunt Mary had taught her last Christmas.

"Over here we have Jill playing the tambourine." Jill shook the tambourine above her head and down by her knees.

"Next is J.R. on the electric guitar." J.R. strummed his guitar and make it quiver.

"And me on the guitar." Becky played a scale.

They began their concert with *The Loco-Motion*. Next was the popular song from The Country Place. They belted out *That's the Way (I Like It)*. Then they hammered out *Bad, Bad, Leroy Brown*.

Becky leaned closer to the microphone. "The last song is for Theron, even though it's a week late," Becky announced.

"Happy birthday to you,

Happy birthday to you,

Happy birthday to Theron,

Happy birthday to you.

And many more!"

Even though the band was questionable, the adults all clapped. They knew the kids had worked hard to prepare for this concert. Leon did that loud whistle between his teeth.

"Hold on, we're not done," J.R. announced. The kids moved the instruments and extension cords to the ground and brought their skateboards to the stage.

Becky stood on the ground with the microphone. "First we have J.R." She held her arm out toward J.R., his cue to begin.

J.R. started at the rear end of the trailer. Mid-way he used his feet to flip the board upside down and back on its wheels then landed on it with both feet and continued rolling.

"And next comes Jill," Becky announced.

They each took a turn showing their families the best tricks they had learned.

The grand finale was all five kids skateboarding in a circle then stopping at the same time, facing the audience in a straight line. They slammed their feet on the back of their skateboards, reached down and grabbed the front with both hand and held them straight up in the air, then lowered them to below their chins.

The adults whistled and clapped.

Yep, Becky thought, *today was a wonderful day. The band, the skateboards and Theron Jon!*